Also by the Author:

No Return
Shower of Stones
Jeroun: The Collected Omnibus

Published by Lethe Press
lethepressbooks.com

Copyright © 2021 Zachary Jernigan
ISBN: 978-1-59021-751-1

Cover artist: Joseph Macalle
Cover design: Inkspiral Design
Typesetting: Ryan Vance

No part of this work may be reproduced or utilized in any form or by any means, electronic or mechanical, including photocopying, microfilm, and recording, or by any information storage and retrieval system, without permission in writing from the Author or Publisher.

This work is fiction, and any resemblance to any real person, dead or otherwise, is incidental

A History of the Defeated

Zachary Jernigan

LETHE PRESS

What do they say? What do they know?
I've been making bad decisions.
   —*B Boys, "Bad Decisions"*

Prota, Medile Sea
(Spring—45 years old—1 year old)

Amur wakes before dawn and sits on the frost-slick porch, naked but unaffected by the cold. Sroma follows him out, yawning and stretching down the steps. She pisses on the turf and curls up next to him, back pressed against his thigh. He watches the glowing curve of the horizon, the farthest edge of the sea.

Soon, details will emerge in the water. The Medile is clear, cold, and shallow. From the bluff the cabin sits upon, he often spots schools of bowfish or goldenalles, a pair of torpaedo hunting—even the occasional oarfish as it migrates north, coiling hugely and languidly up from the icy waters of the Edn.

He presses his hand to Sroma's back. She growls softly, lost in dream. He curves his fingers into her fur, scratching along her spine. He squints, trying to catch the first detail in the water. He misses it, as always. The wrinkles appear in an instant, spreading faster than the eye can follow, an uncountable number etched upon the sea.

The sun peeks over the horizon. Eyes open wide to accept it, Amur stretches his arms above his head, cracks his neck. He massages one heavy pectoral, then the other. He slaps the firm flesh of his thighs and breathes in deeply through the nose, to the belly, throughout the body, before releasing it.

"Hey you. Wake up," he says.

Sroma opens her forge-fire eyes, lifts her head. She yawns and rises to sit, shoulders level with Amur's. For a while she watches the edge of the sun expand. He counts her breaths, listens to them until they take on a keening tone. He chuckles and she huffs. She turns her head toward him, black tongue lolling, steam rising from her open mouth. He cocks his head in time, avoiding the scalding touch of her tongue.

"Yes?" he says, drawing the word out. She stands, panting harder, whining, tale whipping side to side, *thwack thwack thwack* against the porch railings. She pushes her nose into his face; he laughs, pushes her away. "Do you want to go for a r—"

She bolts off the porch, stumbles awkwardly down the rock steps from the bluff, and races toward the shoreline. She wheels about and shakes off her excitement. She starts barking and won't stop barking till he's down there.

With a dramatic groan, he stands. He makes his way down. "Go!" he yells as his feet hit sand. "Get it out of you."

The dog's off down the beach. Amur follows.

Six kilometers to the bay's southern end, six kilometers back, in less than an hour. Few men can run this fast for this long; none can do as Amur does, over sand and rock, barefooted, body dense with muscle. And he's still shedding time.

Sroma has no trouble keeping up. She runs for the joy of it, racing against herself, tearing gouges in the shoreline and throwing up clumps of wet sand. She catapults into the waves. Occasionally she catches a fish and sloppily eats it, bones and all.

Theirs is the island's northernmost property. Merit, a small town, sits two kilometers south along the bay. Twenty or so clapboard houses, a small general store—adequate for the essentials only; for good food or a newsstand, you bike three hours inland. The townspeople generally ignore the tall, naked foreigner and his fearsome pet as they run past. He generally does the same.

One man, old and blind and scarred, spends every day in a rocking chair upon his porch. Every day Amur whistles a hello—a riff from a Tomen anthem popularized in his youth. A celebration of brotherhood, of good food and sex. Shitty song. Hearing it, the old man's frown deepens. Amur smiles and wonders why the dude came here.

"Desert folk like the beach," Dansia told him once. Makes sense, he supposes. He's always loved the sea. The idea of the sea.

Back home, he selects a length of dried boar tendon from the pantry. Drooling puddles on the floor, eyes on his hands the whole way, Sroma stumbles over her feet following him out back. She gnaws for a bit on the tough ligament before snapping it in easy pieces and inhaling it. She collapses on the cool sand. A two-hour nap and she'll want to run again. She'll get hungry and take off for a bit, come back with blood speckling her ruff.

He makes an omelette spiked with a quarter-gram dust. Sroma licks her lips and he snaps his fingers at her—"You had yours." He eats on the porch, listening with half an ear to the soft swirling roar of the record he left half-done on the turntable last night, Cold Pumas *Hanging Valley*, though it may be the first album; he's heard them both so many times it's tough to tell. He watches the tide roll out. He goes back inside and collapses into the old leather armchair.

The dust hits, but softly, coaxing his eyelids down.

He doesn't succumb to sleep; he occupies a space between waking and dream—aware but transfixed, caught, bones vibrating under fast-twitching muscles. He doesn't hate it, though it sometimes go bad. Give it time, relax, he tells himself; you're good.

But it's nothing, really, and he rouses from it quickly; the album's ended and the sun has barely moved across the floorboards. The fingers of his right hand are splayed over the hard ridge of his belly. His left hand descends, finds the painfully erect length of his cock. He strokes himself lazily for a while but dismisses it for later. He sways upon standing, vision blurred by rainbow geometries, ears filled with wyrmsong and the drum of his heart.

The statuette of Vedas upon the bookshelf catches his eye. He picks it up and explores its glossy-black surface with his fingertips. The familiar swells of muscle, the semi-erect penis (of course), the signature on the bottom. *A Ola—spring '198*. A younger Amur ran his fingers over it, the same way. Many times, until he knows its surface this well. He tries to remember one such time. He tries to summon what it was like, being young, creating things. It wasn't that long ago. He remembers some of it, but not the good parts.

("Looks just like you." A man's voice, amused. "You cocky shit." That's it. He doesn't try to summon more.)

He places the statuette back on the bookshelf, just so. He looks at his books. He's read them all, but soon he'll read them again. He looks at his music journals, his art folios. He rarely opens them, some not in years.

His old three-speed leans against the wall, its tires deflated and cracked. He unbuckles a pannier from the frame and breathes in the scent of dirt and sun, beeswax and cotton. He scratches flakes of rust off the headlight, which never worked properly. He's got another bike now, a beefier model better suited to forest roads. Occasionally he thinks about selling the three-speed, but can't make himself do it.

In the backyard, he squats in the sand, lifts a grey stone so large his arms barely encircle it, and tosses it as far as he can. He repeats it until he hates it and wants to die, and moves on, to another equally demanding task. He sprints with another grey stone cradled to his chest. He jumps as high as he can, or leaps great bounding steps, with yet another grey stone. He keeps track on a notepad—the exercise; the size of the stone; distances; and the number of times he can do each till exhaustion. His progress is steady and shows no sign of tailing off.

He earns it. He and the dust earn it. Call it 30-70.

He regards the dog. She's found an enviable position on her back with legs splayed.

"Sure, sure. Sleep off your hard work," he says. She beats her tail against the ground but stays otherwise still. He wipes the sweat from his hairless scalp and flings it at her.

He frowns as he considers the flat, man-sized boulder he'll move from the south end of the backyard to the north. His least favorite exercise, which he leaves till the end, like a fool. By the third pass he's exhausted, coated in sweat and sand, his good will toward even Sroma dissolved. He hates everything, for a bit. He thinks of Dorone, finally, because there's no point in avoiding it. With each heave, he imagines the elderim's body beneath the boulder, crushed.

Following a short swim, he eats his fourth meal, mixing cold rice and minted lamb porridge with another quarter-gram dust. He grimaces through each bite; the dust plays off the mint in an odd way, filling his mouth with the tooth-aching taste of iron.

But the dose hits him on the walk to the glade west of their cabin, and it's good. He grins at his feet as he lifts them high, marveling at the springiness of his legs; for several seconds he simply stands with his right foot in the air—perplexed at how it came to be that he's standing here, in the forest beyond the meadow behind his cabin, aracora swaying gently in the breeze around him, with a foot in the air.

"One jump," he whispers, and he can break free of the world's embrace.

He continues. As he nears the break in the trees, a pressure fills his chest. He breathes heavily. Tears spill from his eyes, running coldly down his cheeks, as he steps among the wooden dummies positioned in the center of the glade. Blinking away the vision before him—not dummies but elderim; *one* elderim, repeated—he stands like he's been caught unprepared, weight shifting to one foot then the other. He winces as though struck; he pulls back like someone's kissed him without his say-so.

Sometimes he meditates first; he seeks a center away from his rage before inevitably finding it again. Not today. He spins on his foot clockwise, right arm extended. *Crack*, the closest dummy's central pole fractures, top to bottom. Sroma, a predatory shadow lounging at the border of trees and grass, twitches her ears, goes back to sleep.

Amur trains. He starts with slower movements, methodical, soft strikes against the dummies' arms and legs, before moving on to swfiter, more complex maneuvers. His arms blur; he pivots between dummies as though he's fighting multiple men. Wood begins to crack under the onslaught. In the final minutes, he reduces the dummies to splinters and envisions: Not wood, but flesh. His enemy has fallen, is pulped under his fists, stamped into red paste under his feet. He does briefly think of sex; there's no avoiding it. He rises from his knees, blood dripping from the mangled mess of his knuckles. The air smells of blood and sweat and pine sap. He and the dog stare at each other, panting.

"Dorone," Amur says. "Dorone. *Bad*."

She sniffs the air and huffs, hackles raised. He nods and retrieves his saw from its stump. For the next three hours he cuts limbs from the forest and carries them back home. He'll spend two days building new dummies to be destroyed in less time than it takes to make a good meal.

Then again. And again.

After training and Sroma's play is done, they sit at the tideline, watching Fyra and Berun rise over the sea. "Must be the brightest night of the year," he says to her. What a dumb thing to say, he thinks. He tips his head side to side. "It was bright out yesterday, too." The air smells of salt and life and he's drunk.

Thinking of his mothers—well, Chora—he touches his right index finger and thumb to his temple and mouths, *Vedas be with you*. Real slowly, perfect pronunciation, like they teach you at temple. With his other hand, he strokes Sroma's forehead, scratches behind her ears. She clumsily lays most of herself in his lap. She snuffles for a bit in her crotch and then spends what feels like ten minutes readjusting her head in his lap, finally pushing her hot, wet nose into the crevice of his knee. He examines his split knuckles. As he watches, one wound closes, puckering out a splinter of pale wood or bone.

Chora would hate *that*, he thinks. He frowns.

"I'm forgetting what they look like," he says, but he doesn't imagine either of them, not even Chora, even for a second. Pressing too hard hastens the erasure, the forgetting. That's how he lost Agra. Her name escapes him sometimes now.

It *is* Agra, though. He isn't always sure. She loved cats.

"I know, I know, I know. I *know*. You've heard it before. You've heard it *all* before."

Sroma opens one eye, spilling red light onto the sand. He flaps her ear back and forth until she moans testily and nips at his calf. He chuckles sorry.

"I prepared for it. I guess I thought I did. I mean, if I'm going to be this thing—" he grabs his pec "—hanging around this thing—" he pets her back softly "—then I must give some things up. I'm *good* at giving things up. But seriously, how can you prepare for that?" He shakes his head, feeling foolish (like someone's watching *his* behavior, way out here) but not caring overmuch. She likes the sound of his voice and he wants to talk. He wants to smile instead of frown, and not just because of her. "I'm still not sure what the hell I'm doing." He fills his lungs, makes his voice grand and deep. "But did any of our heroes know what they were doing? Did Vedas know? Of course not! He survived on his wits, his strength and speed. I am the same. *Take care of her!* your papa told me! And I will."

The moons rise while he tells her old tales, good Nosi adventures. He doesn't worry about losing them because there's no pushing involved—he doesn't try to remember what's right and wrong, what names he's messed up; he just rambles like he's listening to someone else tell a story. Because there *are* still stories, some that make him laugh out loud to tell, even to a dog. There's one about her, the Hound, killing and eating people, a demon let loose on the world. It's a real story and it isn't, somehow, with her.

"You never *ate* anyone, did you?" He leans over and buries his nose in the thick fur of her neck, breathing in her musky saltwater scent. "No, not *you*. Some other *naughty* dog."

He uncorks his beer and downs half before coming up for air. He burps, long and satisfyingly, and kills the rest a little slower. A large crab sidles nearby and he flings the bottle, hitting the creature squarely, cracking its carapace open.

He winces; he didn't mean to hit it. They taste like shit.

"Birdfood," he says and falls back, staring into the sky.

Sroma snores but abruptly raises her head when one of their neighbor's dogs barks. A rumble builds in her chest. The dog barks again. Another of its mates joins in with a higher yip. Sroma growls. A Stoli couple live half a kilometer inland, on a large property. Their dogs don't venture off grounds. Best for them, though in truth Sroma acts around domesticated dogs like a lion does around kitty cats—who gives a shit about *these* things, you know?

Amur grabs Sroma's jowls and pulls her face to his. She pulls away, twitching to run. Her expression, suddenly puppyish.

"Go. Rip their throats out," he tells her.

Instead, she retrieves the crab and drops it at his feet. He reaches for the second beer, this one brewed with a sixteenth-gram dust. He pushes her away; she's always trying to get at anything with dust in it.

The neighbor's dogs continue their noise, agitated by who knows what. They pause for a while, and Amur thinks they may have quit, before they take up the racket again. He leans back on his elbows and admires Sroma's profile against the starshot sky. He considers how she may die, how he may die. He thinks of Dorone, but oddly of their tenderness. He was such a fool. He *is* such a fool.

"You know, I used to think I didn't like dogs."

She's heard it before.

Kua, Semet al-E, Southern Ob, Iswee
(Fall—22 years old)

The sky is blue-green and cloudless. The water hisses as it laps the shore. Bright fish dart in the shallows.

Amur walks along the tideline, small brittle shells and smooth stones crunching under his feet. His hair is bushier than he prefers—the salt and sun is drying it out, turning it white and *only* white, no shimmer or nuance at all. He wears a short multicolored wrap, cinched low and tight on his hips, accentuating his ass. On his left wrist is a bracelet of stone beads, a shade of pink new to him, so bright it seems to glow. On his right is Dorone's first gift, a perpetually ticking, ever-precise watch worth more than his mothers' home.

Since leaving the Continent two months ago, he has eschewed any other jewelry, and his ears feel most naked. He wants to tug on them, stretching the holes to keep them open. He doesn't. He stopped after Dorone said something about it. Not something unkind, just something.

Dorone walks beside him, naked as is typical for someone of his age and status. Half a hand taller than Amur, thinner but more densely muscled, he moves like a fighter, like a dancer. His lavender skin gleams as though polished. His teeth flash like bleached coral, perfectly straight; they are sharper and more numerous than a man's.

His left arm is sheathed from mid-bicep to fingertip in the deep blue scales of his armor. Though Amur loves Dorone's looks, he wouldn't love them nearly as much without the armor. The Elder relic conforms to his lover like a second skin, highlighting his musculature rather than obscuring it. Its colors shift subtly, deep and rich within a narrow spectrum, depending on the light, the angle. Amur loves best the feel of it, cold and smooth and scaled like snakeskin, utterly impregnable and alien. The border between it and Dorone's skin is imperceptible, as though the relic has fused to him at the cellular level. At Dorone's slightest command it moves upon his body, covering more territory.

To feel it move under your skin. Under your hips. Amur has several complex fantasies about it. Dozens. And more acted out each day.

"Lovely day, no?" Dorone says.

Amur stares at his lover's elegant profile, set against the diamond sea. Dorone turns to him and winks. The deep wrinkles around his amber cat-eyes, the tips of his perfectly formed ears, the stylishly windswept silver wave of his hair—he's as much art as creature, and for a moment Amur forgets. He takes Dorone's hand and nearly suggests an early lunch.

"We got a couple spies," Orrus says, pointing. "Heyo, there! We see you."

In the tall grasses above the beach, two elderim boys stand. They laugh and wave and take flight toward the whitewashed city overlooking the bay. Dorone guffaws and pulls Amur into an embrace. "Happens everywhere we go, doesn't it?" he says, grinning like a kid even though it happens wherever he and Amur go. It's the show of it. He places his unarmored hand on the back of Amur's neck. Amur smiles into the kiss, but his mood is soured and it's got nothing to do with the gawkers.

The other elderim, the Hound. The reason they're all here.

Orrus shakes his head with an amused expression and continues walking. He's Dorone's contemporary, just past middle age but not out of his prime—eleven or twelve hundred years old, maybe even closing in on thirteen. The perfection of his body, its powerful yet elegant musculature, is a foregone conclusion. His cock is larger than Dorone's, thicker but in Amur's opinion less beautiful. He's taller and looser limbed than Dorone, though; he ambles where his prince strides, with the slightest habitual slouch in the shoulders. He's paler skinned and in Amur's eyes far less perfect.

He's not without a rangy charisma, though. Like all of his people, he is poised, measured of speech, though his expressions are a tad languid for Amur, as though he's apathetic or unwatchful—which of course he isn't. His eyes are two different shades of dull gold, and the tip of his left ear is missing, the scar puckered as though the flesh was torn rather than cut. His hair is cut expertly, calculated to look like fabulous bedhead. Its color is Amur's least favorite shade of red, like a certain type of dying leaf from a tree whose name escapes him.

On Orrus, it's dazzling.

His armor is formed into broad bands of matte gold around left bicep and right thigh, accentuating the flexion of muscle underneath. Amur is dying to feel it; it looks something like the fabric Agra found near the river when they were kids. Of course they believed it was elderim stuff. He used to put it to his lips, to his thighs. His first erection.

As commanded, Orrus has brought the Hound, which he calls Sroma. Her fierce head comes to Amur's chin. Her eyes glow with a baleful fire even in daylight. Her tongue is hot enough to redden the skin. Otherwise, she seems to Amur like any other dog, bothersome and undignified. She runs upshore, races back, and leaps into the sea, shattering its cerulean calm. Orrus greets her with laughter and a slap on the rump.

When she comes up to Amur, black tongue dripping and steaming, he pats her head and scratches behind her ears. Her fur is softer than he imagined. He isn't nervous, not particularly. He's confident around animals, and it's all too easy to believe she's a normal animal, to forget what's going on.

"Good girl," he says to her, firmly but softly, like he needs to be polite. "Go away. *Go*."

She huffs hot snot into his face and runs off.

She won't approach Dorone.

A day before Orrus was to arrive in Kua, Dorone took him to the Elder city Sispun, a day's travel east by aircar into Southern Ob's hill country. After dinner, he told Amur about Orrus and the Hound. It struck Amur as preposterous, that Dorone himself would mete out this justice. And he didn't like the way Dorone put it, the way he thought about the whole thing: *I'm doing this for you, Amur*. As if he should appreciate this gesture. It meant nothing, nothing. *Is there still a war on? Is the Hound still killing us? It's a dog, Dorone. I don't understand.*

"I think it's fitting," Dorone said, managing to look crestfallen as he swirled the remainder of his vegetables around his plate. Greens; Dorone didn't like greens. "I thought you'd understand and approve, even show some *enthusiasm*. For goodness sake, this is diplomacy, Amur, with your government. This is for you, for your people. I've arranged this with Solwan, with her interior secretary, at great cost. Surely you know the story? The Hound? You must!"

"Of course I do," Amur snapped. "I'm not simple, Dorone. It's a kids story. I know it's a *fucking fact*. I do, okay? I just don't get it, and why it must be together. I don't want to see it."

Dorone held up his hands. "All right. And I understand. But this must be done, and I want you there with me, for *my* sake, for the weight of my conscience, which I don't need to remind you is qu—" He read Amur's expression and sighed. "There's no danger to you or me. But I have sympathy for Orrus. He loves her dearly. They've been together for centuries. He'll act like it doesn't matter as long as he can. I won't like him very much then, *or* when he's honest with me." He frowned theatrically. "I haven't liked him in some time, in fact."

Amur laughed. "*He'll* act that way! You'll act that way, too. You all do. You can't just fucking *talk* to each other, not even about something like this."

"What an expert you are already! His feelings must be preserved."

"Preserved!" Amur pointed his steak knife across the table at Dorone. "He's hundreds of years old. Oh, sorry; *thousands*. Yes, I know. *I'm* the young one. I understand. I get it. That's another thing, though." He held his finger in the air—his *lecturing pose*, his sisters called it. "I only like you and the kids around here. I just… I don't get them. Adults here. They're never talking to me. Oh, they're charming and they're never done with the compliments, but they're not looking at me, you know?"

"No, I don't." Dorone said. He frowned and shook his head. "No, that's not true. I do, I get it. I've lived with your people, Amur. Most of us haven't. We've forgotten."

"What does that mean? Who's going to remind them?"

Dorone stared at him. "Are we going to talk about Orrus? This is important."

Amur stood, crossed the suite floor to Dorone at the bar. He selected a joint and lit it. "I do feel like a kid here," he said through a cloud of smoke. He stabbed the air between them with the lit end. "Around *you*, most of all, sometimes. I'm no child, Dorone. I get the larger issues, as well as I can." He laughed and it sounded a bit manic. "Is it so odd, love, that I don't want to see you kill a dog?"

Dorone closed his eyes for a bit. Amur stared around their suite, marvelling again at its precise, austere beauty. Suddenly Dorone stood, took Amur's hand, and led him to the fortieth-story balcony overlooking the city. "Tell me what you see," he said.

Amur wrapped his fingers around the iron railing and leaned out. Far below them, past the forest of juniper separating their hilled residence from the rest of Sispun, the city spread in concentric circles around them, each circle ticking like a clock set to a different measurement of time. Ornamented cement-and-glass buildings rumbled past one another, streets constantly reconfiguring. Only the palace in which they stayed remained fixed. The city was empty but furnished, as though its residents had taken off for the day. Come night, lamps lit themselves in buildings, along streets. Hearths sprung alchymical flames to heat no one.

"I see an empty, enchanted city of a race long since gone, of which there must be at least a dozen in Iswee," Amur said. He grinned as Dorone sighed. "Fine. I see far more than that, and it's wonderful and overwhelmingly brilliant, I wish I could stay here forever, but fundamentally that's what it is. A city, empty." He lifted a white eyebrow. "It's the emptiness, love, that appeals to me."

A small lie, not about the emptiness but the city itself. That it was beautiful couldn't be denied, but he preferred Kua, with its tall white elderim buildings stacked atop one another on the hills overlooking the sea, far more than the great ticking and crystalline opulence of the more famous Elder cities like Sispun, where everything was just a tad too tall, too wide, for either man or elderim.

Dorone groaned and pinched Amur's ass hard enough to make him yelp. "By empty, you mean abandoned. Perfectly good city, no one lives here anymore. You've been to Huad and Ladrelee, Amur—my people live in those cities, don't we?"

Amur turned his back to the view and leaned against the railing. Taking a long drag, he shrugged. "You people are weird. You do weird things." He laughed out loud at the next thought: "I mean, look at who your parents are."

Dorone rolled his eyes, leaned his arms on the railing, and Amur admired the arc of his body, the precise lines of his musculature. His hips, particularly, the cleft of shadow between the curve of butt cheek and the swell of hip bone. For the hundredth time, Amur's fingers itched for a pen to capture his lover's construction. He suppressed the urge. Somehow, he never did it. The thought of asking Dorone to pose horrified him, and Dorone never offered. Amur wanted him to offer.

He loosened his wrap, let it fall to the floor. He gripped it with his toes and flicked it across the flagstones. He stroked his cock. Why were they talking about this?

Dorone had turned to watch him. "Youth! You know so little and say it with such confidence. *Weird*, you say. We aren't like your people, yes. It will be centuries before we can share Jeroun like one people again—*no*, don't ask me why it must take so long, not that conversation *again*, Amur. But we have curiosity! *You* haven't even asked how long this place has been abandoned. Aren't you curious, Amur? This place was ancient before the advent of men."

"Yes," Amur lied. It hadn't occurred to him to wonder. Iswee belonged to the elderim and always had. Prior to that, in incomprehensibly remote days, it belonged to the Elder themselves. That's why he preferred cities like Kua; perfect as they were, the elderim hadn't just inherited them like they'd inherited everything else of great value in the world.

He didn't want to *think* about any of it. He wanted to see it, touch it. He wanted to be with Dorone in beautiful places men rarely see, preferably just the two of them alone. The parties were tiring him. Not so much to ask.

Dorone traced a fingertip along Amur's jawline. He had that look in his eyes; *You will listen now.* It thrilled Amur as much as it annoyed him, that look. The power of his erection shocked him. Dorone looked down at it, but didn't move his hand.

"It's nice to act as lovers do in your romantic novels, as equals, Amur. I've fought the urge to reveal the extent of my influence to you, but I *am* this creature, of this influence, and I like grand gestures." He turned back to the city revolving around them, holding his arms out as though he could hold the whole place. "I ordered Sispun emptied for our arrival."

Amur crossed his arms. He stared at the crumpled ball of his wrap, half on the marble of the apartment, half on the flagstones of the balcony. He tensed to retrieve it.

Dorone placed his hand on Amur's arm. "These gestures bother you. But I know I've asked a lot. It's a gift, and it's nothing, love—nothing at all. It's expected of me."

Amur lifted his chin imperiously. "When you were young, did you occasionally do the *unexpected*, or does advanced age have nothing to do with it?"

"Gah!" Dorone yelled. He leaned over and pantomimed pulling a knife from his back. He took hold of Amur's arm and pulled him close, cupping his ass. Amur slipped a hand between them, took Dorone's cock in his calloused grip.

Amur bit Dorone's ear. "But really. Why do it, love? It's not *that* hard to find solitude."

Dorone pulled Amur's hips in tight, trapping his arm between them. "Because I can, and because you deserve it. Because I wanted us to be *alone* alone, completely."

Amur smiled as Dorone laid him on the flagstones. He shivered at the coldness and spread his legs. He panted and groaned, grinding against Dorone's erection, already begging please. Dorone stopped, spit in his palm. ("Elderim spit is ideal for this," Dorone told him early on. Some gibberish about fats and acids; Amur wasn't listening because he wanted Dorone so badly.) He gasped, fingernails biting into the hard flesh of Dorone's shoulders as Dorone thrust, slowly but inexorably, into him. The whole fucking thing was uncomfortable—the position, the flagstones, Dorone's size—and it drove him mad with want; he hooked his heels under Dorone's buttocks and pulled him deeper. "Faster," he said, watching the armor as it moved over Dorone, scales flowing like fluid over his lover's taut skin. He begged and begged, for what he didn't know, and soon lost control of himself and came, without a stroke or a tug, legs shaking, heels pounding Dorone's back, spurting onto his own chest and face.

Dorone came above him, teeth clenched in ecstasy, blue light spilling from his eyes.

Amur took a long bath, lit another joint, and found Dorone sitting with his back against the railing, the city spread out far below, a trio of white owls doing acrobatics in the night sky beyond. (City of Owls—another name for Sispun. These places were all so beautiful and poetic. He compared them to home. It made him angry.) He leaned into the heat of his lover's naked body and was struck, not for the first time, that Dorone wasn't so much bigger than him. He'd faced men taller and heavier. Men.

Dorone breathed in and Amur tensed. The quiet was so nice. "I'm not *killing* her. I am her natural master, not Orrus. She won't feel a thing."

"She?"

"As I understand. I don't care for dogs. If it'd been a cat, *well* then." He wrapped his arms around Amur's belly and squeezed tight before letting go. "We should stop talking about this."

Amur agreed. Regardless: "You talk about my people, though, about justice. Is this a real thing, Dorone? Or is it just a gesture?"

"It's real."

"It won't feel a thing? It'll be..."

"Peaceful, Amur. On my honor."

"And he won't run? You say he loves it. Her. *Loves*."

"He'll come by my bidding."

Amur shifted his hips, grinding softly against Dorone's hardening erection. The air smelled of pine and sex. He reached his hand back to run his fingers through Dorone's ridiculously touchable hair; he rubbed the tip of Dorone's ear.

"And do I come by your bidding?"

Dorone paused. When he spoke, Amur heard no trace of a smile. "No. You've always had a choice."

Prota, Medile Sea
(Fall—46 years old—2 years old)

One day each week he relents, roughhousing with her until she's exhausted or he can take no more.

He gives no hint until after lunch, when the jittery high of the dust—a slightly higher dose than normal—has worn off. Walking through the meadow toward the woods out back, he suddenly stops. She huffs and nearly collides with him. He turns around and smiles. Her mouth drops open to pant. "Okay, come on," he says a heartbeat before she barrels into his chest, knocking him to the ground.

They wrestle. Amur holds back nothing for fear of hurting her. Regardless of what the dust has done, he is severely outclassed; she can kill him if she chooses, surely. (Looking at her spread out on the floor: "Vedas Tezul, girl, you're huge.") Her teeth tear, her mouth scalds, her iron-hard skull nearly concusses; he keeps his fingers from being nipped off, but only just. She gouges his arms and legs with her claws, pausing to lap at his blood. She pants, grins, and licks his face before resuming their play. He laughs but there's fear in it. The blood makes her eyes go a bit wild; she's overjoyed and unpredictable.

"Okay, okay," he says finally, hands up and waving. She's outlasted him.

"All done." She nips at his face. "*All done.*" She grins, tongue flapping spittle, and jumps off him. "Good girl."

Laying here in the sand, smiling, great chest heaving, wounds stitching closed—it's *much* worse than last time. A hundred needles, pain and itch multiplied a hundredfold. He faces it, knowing how temporary pain is. He's always been strong.

Sroma gives him maybe five minutes and then tears past him toward the sea. Amur groans. She reaches the shore and starts barking, like she always does, not stopping until he starts down the stairs cut into the bluff, at which point she'll freak the fuck out with excitement. Still such a puppy. He rises and stretches, his abused body protesting; a couple newly sealed wounds split back open.

His heart quickens again and the dust responds. He roars his challenge to her, back arched as his lungs clear. Empty boast; he has no shot of catching her. He races down the steps, though, and gives good chase. Keeping just ahead of him, she lets his fingertips brush her hindquarters before she sprints away. Three times, up and down their stretch of beach. He admires her, the way she holds nothing back.

She wheels about, drops the branch. Her tongue flaps out the side of her long, tooth-lined jaws. "Back," he says. She crouches low on her forelegs. He gestures impatiently—"Get back, I said. *Back*. Make it fair. *Sroma!*" She scoots away from the branch, backside swaying like mad to the wagging of her tail.

"One. Two..."

He sprints three times faster than a normal man and still gets there too late. As she spins away, however, he gets a grip on her left hind leg. She turns in an instant, snarling, and clamps her jaws around his forearm. They crash into the sand and he lets go.

Blood wells, spilling to the sand. The flow stops quickly, but his hand won't flex upward and his fingers won't quite close. He palpates his forearm, closer to the elbow. There, the bulge of one or two severed tendons.

"Fuck." Maybe a day lost while it heals. A painful, painful heal.

Sroma cares nothing for his injury. She barks, impatient with his shit. He shakes his head, sets off after her.

The ruins of Qemet sit upon the rocky, northernmost tip of the island, a two-kilometer trek from the cabin. Locals rarely visit the place—out of disinterest or fear of the statues, that one place where a bit of Elder magic still exists on the island, Amur neither knows nor cares.

They take a leisurely walk there after dinner. The air smells like rain, like the changing of seasons. Reaching the first stretch of stone road, Sroma sprints off. Chicken-sized lizards scamper. All kinds of reptiles live on the island, but Sroma prefers the toothy cat-sized ones that sun themselves on the city's stone walls. She kills them, however many she can catch, and doesn't eat even one. He leaves her to it, and follows a tilted flagstone path around the wind and rain eroded ruins. The ancient seawall is falling into the sea; he hops from rock to rock, over waves as the tide presses in. He sits on the largest, northernmost stone, peering at the grey clouds rising just beyond the horizon.

When the tideline is quite high he hops back and enters the city. Sroma finds him, burns his face with her tongue, and bounds off again through roofless interiors. Amur walks to the central square, with its statue of Adrash.

The god stands upon a column of black marble veined with pale blue. His posture is relaxed yet ready, hands open at his waist. His proportions are those of a man in his athletic prime. His body is carved from granaust, a radiantly white stone — an unusual choice, for Adrash is rarely portrayed in his armor; he is typically naked, black skinned, the armor a stamp upon his chest or an abstract design upon his body.

Amur stares at the god's cock and balls, cradled by the armor's embrace, and admires the artist's skill in capturing such a nuanced effect. Not for the first time, he nearly convinces himself to climb the column and examine the statue more closely—understand it with his own hands. He imagines pressing himself to it, letting his cock grow hard against the swells of its cold, hard buttocks.

To think that he didn't know of its existence when he chose this place—this island, and then his cabin so close to it! According to the book he bought in Etche, it was commissioned during Adrash's lifetime, nearly twenty thousand years ago. An inconceivable amount of time. The fact that it exists, here in this faraway place with so few people knowing, so few people ever seeing, stuns him. He reminds himself that rocks are old, too. Adrash is *gone* gone; not even the elderim give a damn about some unreturned god. *Stories* are better than that.

But there is Elder magic here, some relic buried deep inside or incorporated into the stone—of this he is certain. The statue appears as though it was unveiled yesterday. Birds don't shit on it. Staring into its gold leaf-covered eyes, Amur fights the urge to kneel and explain his presence here. And when Sroma skids into the plaza, she growls at the statue, like she's done each time before, hackles up, muzzle down. Her legs shake as she lowers her butt to the ground. She growls deep in her throat and places her head under Amur's palm.

He runs his hands over the contours of his own body. He's not so different in form or feature from the god. Heavy doses of dust have erased forty-six years of wrinkles and scars, leaving his skin as smooth as stone, as lustrous as polished onyx. He takes his cock and balls in his fist, imagining the god's armor flowing over them, cupping them. He imagines the armor slipping cool and liquid over his chest, his belly—being covered, consumed. He imagines having it for himself, the most potent relic of all. *The* armor.

He stares at the statue's gold leaf-covered eyes. Thinking-not-thinking of Chora, he touches his right index finger and thumb to his temple.

"Vedas be with you," he says.

He decides he'll take a piss at the base of the fountain; he's always wanted to and stopped himself, like someone's watching. The flow starts, and his vision shudders. A wave of nausea passes through him, and there's an unpleasant ringing in his ears, but he sticks it out, pushing until his bladder is empty. Turning his back to the statue takes effort.

Whining, quivering like she's palsied, Sroma steps forward to sniff at the column. She crouches and pisses too.

—oh so briefly! She's already off, head held high like she's conquered a dragon.

Amur claps his hands and whoops. "You left more *drool* on the ground! *Seriously*, girl!"

Rain clouds rise over the sea on their return. Staring at the oncoming mountains of grey, Amur lets a somber mood overtake him. Sroma veers into him and whines, pushing her head against his arm. He stoops to retrieve a length of driftwood. "Go," he tells her, hurling it down the beach, wincing at the flare of pain in his wrist. "Keep away." She jumps forward, stops herself. Occasionally she trots ahead or swerves into the surf for a drink of water—the salt has never turned her off—but her attention rarely strays from him. He reads concern on her face, in her eyes. "I'm fine," he says. "No need to worry. Run. Go." She stays with him. When he stops, she stops. When he turns to the sea, she turns to the sea. She flinches when the clouds strobe, the sky cracks and tears. He pats her shoulders.

They reach home just as the sheets come down, saturating the sand, carving rivers through the beach to the churning waves. The light he left on in the cabin is out. They lose power in every storm. He remains outside but opens the door for Sroma to scamper in. Odd to see her enormous, long-legged body scamper. Odd to see the nose of that wolf head pressed to the rattan screen, those smoldering eyes wide with fear.

"Lager *one*," he says. She pads off; he hears her open the icebox door with her nose; she returns with a bottle in her jaws. When he opens the door to retrieve it, she steps halfway across the threshold. He takes the beer and waits patiently. The sky erupts in light and thunder. She backs into the cabin. "Next time," he says. Sitting cross-legged on the porch, he uncorks the bottle and takes a swig of the dusted brew. He grins and takes a big swig.

Oh, so quick this time. Only a handful of heartbeats pass before the warmth hits, flowing giddily through his veins. Pressure builds in his ears.

"Oh. *Oh*," he says, pressing his hands to the floor to stay anchored, to keep from floating into the sky. "*Mmmm*," he groans, shutting his eyes tight. The dust is unpredictable. One out of every dozen doses throws him. He shudders, head to toe, muscles flexing and slackening to the dust's rhythm. There's intent to it; the dust says *look what I can make you feel*. He clenches his fists until his finger bones creak. He shuts his eyes. A webwork of light pulses at the edges of them, reaching thin tendrils across the dark span, linking briefly before dissipating. There are shapes and figures; there are no shapes or figures. But violence—there's that, and it's everything there is until there's no more room for *seeing* anything; it's the sound of earthquakes and landslides; it's the sound of icebergs calving. Something huge lumbers by, its growls reverberating through him. Finally it's waves and it's rain, breaking against the shores of his eardrums, an echoing chorus of shouts, falling on the earth of his mind, a deluge of plainspoken but angry alien words.

The tide turns suddenly, and who knows why. His erection is sudden, painful. He comes, spurting onto the porch. Again, and then a third time; the pleasure radiates through his body, echoes upon echoes undiminished. When it becomes too much, an overabundance of pleasure threatening to pain, he opens his eyes onto a world that glows, that crackles around the edges. He smiles wide as a gust of wind sends a sheet of water against the porch, soaking him. He tastes, though his skin, the freshness of the storm and the salt of his sweat.

Gradually, smile turns to grimace. His body is ill equipped to feel all at once, every nerve tuned to the infinite. The lightning flashes unceasingly, filling his skull with light, with static. The thunder reverberates in his bones, rebounds, resounds again. A shudder moves through him, like sound through thin glass; he is a container, that is all; he will shatter or he will overflow with light and sound. He will explode. He will collapse.

Sroma, giddy with the scent of the dust, snuffles loudly behind the screen.

"Not for you," he says, each word drawn out into a ridiculous slurring echo. "You. You're strong enough *aaasss iiiiiiisssssss.*" She whines, on and on and on and on *on on on*...

The dust *shifts* within him. Perception snaps back into focus. He gasps, blinking into a dimmer, smaller world. He *gets* it; he can fit the whole of Jeroun between his hands. He downs the rest of the beer, knowing now the acclimation will be swifter.

The second dose hits, quickening in his veins, jolting him to his feet. He grins with aching jaws, vibrating teeth. He sprints to the edge of the bluff and leaps, landing hip deep in the shallows twenty meters below. He runs, shins slicing through the water as though it were air.

He stops and roars. Behind him, Sroma howls. A desperate sound.

He counts, *one, two, three...*

The screen door slams open, probably off its hinges. The dog gives chase.

He admits it to himself, for he is the kind of man whose mind demands clarity. When he admits it, it makes him afraid.

He loves her a great deal, more perhaps than he's loved anything. Definitely more. He thinks about how love has ruined him twice, maybe more, definitely more. He thinks about a boy and a dog; he's certain there was a boy and a dog, and that it doesn't end well. He thinks about Orrus: how his plan failed, how time may prove him wrong about everything. He thinks about what Orrus meant to do—what he *believed* he could do, and how that influenced the way he spoke to Amur, with such confidence.

But Dorone lived! He lived.

He thinks about it again, like there's something to work out after all this time, like thinking about it has ever changed a fucking thing.

"He'll find it if I take it."
"He won't," Orrus says.
"He'll find her if I take it."

"He won't," Orrus says.
"He'll find her."
"He won't."

When he can't handle it anymore, he finds Sroma wherever she is and bugs her. He sits down next to her and pets her, or he takes her for a walk. He remembers his breathing, and to pay attention to what's going on right now. Sometimes he thinks about drawing her. He never does. No one to see it.

(Agra. Agra likes animals. ... That's it.)

He won't allow her to sleep on the bed with him because she's gotten too big. She sleeps next to him, on the sheepskin-piled sling bed he made for her. *Mostly*, she sleeps on it; as time passes, she moves more of her body—a foot at first, then a whole leg, occasionally now her head—onto his bed. He chuckles and lets her do it. He can't imagine always telling her what to do.

Now and then, dust and exhaustion aren't enough. He gives up trying, takes a piss, and smokes half a joint sitting in the darkened main room. He picks at a tear in the cracked, sweat-stained armchair, thinking about how it'll one day fall apart; there will be no more chair, no more sweat stains, no more of his ass-stink. He turns on the reading lamp; he turns it off. He gets up to open the shutters and stands in the breeze, goosebumps patterning him in the moonlight. He stares at Berun and Fyra poised over the sea, then turns the lamp back on.

Sitting cross-legged on the floor, he flips through a folio of sketches. His own, '218-19. So recent; he was still doing it then? And they're good. He should've kept more of them.

He shuts the folio before the last few pages because he doesn't want to see it end. He places it back with the other journals and folios. He glares at them. The familiar thought—he'll gather them up, everything he still has, and light a big bonfire on the beach.

The creak of Sroma's bed, the *click-clack* of her nails on the wood floor. "Hey," he says softly. She pads over, tired-footed, and tries to lay her entire body in his lap. He moves her around until her head is nestled in the crook of his knee. He strokes her forehead, massages the velvet tips of her ears. She blinks, staring up at him, eyes dimmed to an amber glow. After a while, she inhales in that way she does: *I'm going to whine softly now.*

"Yeah," he says. "Okay. Let's go back."

Still unable to sleep, the dust whispers, *Now.*

For a time, it's bad. He spreads his arm wide, gripping the edges of the mattress. He shuts his eyes tight like a child, because he knows now that the world has passed on without him. His people, *every* people, the elderim—they've off and gone, along with everything they touched. His homeland, gone. All of the Continent, replaced with sea. Iswee and all the islands thrusting above the waves, all that land clinging to life alone amidst all that water, replaced with sea. Beyond the shore of this one remaining bit of rock and sand, there's nothing but sea.

Then, even the sea goes away. The ground beneath it disappears, and the ground beneath that, and all the layers of heavens and hells. Nothingness eats the world's heart. Only the cabin remains, floating above a memory of a world.

He inhales sharply, heart tugged upward until it presses against his ribs. His body follows, arcing up from the mattress, muscles tensed to wood, to rock, to steel. He gasps through the clenched gristle of his throat and maybe he says *mama*.

Sroma barks, breaking him out of it. The arch of bone and muscle collapses onto the bed, blood pounding through it.

She licks his face; he allows it briefly and then gently pushes her away. "I'm fine. We're fine. Leave me be. Go to sleep." She stares at him in the odd way of hers, calculation in her eyes; she is to normal dogs as Dorone is to mortal men. Maybe. Or she's just a bit *more* of a dog than most. She huffs and drops her head back onto the bed.

He lays one fist under his neck. Knuckles digging into the knotted strands of muscle, he breathes deep into his belly, holds it there for a long while, staring out the window—a portion of the Arc, densely starred, a wisp of cloud lighter in the southeast. He breathes out.

"Okin," he says. "Okin, that's it. *Hoo* boy, was she rough. My other mama, she was always kind. Not smart, but kind. Couldn't avoid getting knocked around by… *fuck*—couldn't help getting hurt by everything, Chora. Chora. And I didn't do anything, nothing, because what am I supposed to do, only son. But *you*, you I can handle. Can I? I can, yes, yes I can…"

Sroma sighs but doesn't raise her head as he talks; he runs his fingertips through the fur of her chest. He starts crying, and cries for a good while. His speech slows and fragments even more. His thoughts are sliced in half, frayed at every edge. Warmth suffuses him from the heart out. Wounds heal. Muscles and bones stitch together, stronger than they were yesterday.

Kua, Semet al-E, Southern Ob, Iswee
(Fall '199—22 years old)

"How much further to this island?" Amur asks. It may be the second time he's asked; he's not sure.

"Just a bit," Dorone answers.

Yes. Second time, same answer. Amur reminds himself to unclench his fists. He thinks of Agra, which always makes him smile. He imagines her playing fetch with the Hound. He wonders why it's so important to smile right now. He can act like a man. There's no rule against it.

Dorone takes his time. He seems to enjoy himself. He stops to angle his sculpted head to the sun, drinking its warmth. He veers Amur into the shallows to look at iridescent crabs. He's an expert shot, his throwing arm a blur. Amur loses sight of his skipped stones long before they stop skipping.

Charmed by his lover despite himself, Amur summons patience. He thinks of justice; surely he can wait, let these odd people do whatever this is, their way.

And, as Dorone predicted, Orrus acts content to stop with them, to also act gay and curious, a morning walk on the beach. He whistles appreciatively when Dorone throws a piece of driftwood into the sky, clipping the tail feathers of a blue gull. "Almost," he says, and knocks the bird from the sky with a pebble. He winks at Amur. The Hound catapults into the water to retrieve her master's kill. When her mouth hits the water, steam billows.

Dorone laughs, and Orrus turns his attention to Amur.

"You study *art* at university!" he proclaims. He looks Amur up and down in a way Amur finds uncouth. Amur is either extremely pretty or ugly here, depending on the person. Either way, he never feels like a man should, among men. Of course he doesn't. The idea he *can* is preposterous. "I'd love to see some of your work. I collect art, mostly modern but some classical. Have you heard of Norrvide? What about Rahbek?" He waves his hands. "Nevermind. Where were you born?"

"In Jalast," Amur answers. "My family's always been there."

"Ah, yes. People of the Mesa, Blessed of Vedas. Beautiful country." Orrus smiles dazzlingly. "Yes, I'm familiar. I toured the region many times, before you were born. Long time ago." He gives Amur yet another appraising look. "I can see why you caught his eye. He's always had good taste. You needn't wear clothes, you know. The status laws don't apply to you." He laughs. "It's not like you'll *burn*, boy."

A fist forms in Amur's throat, squeezing. He opens his mouth, shuts it. Orrus talks like most of them do—the adults, at least. Like Amur can't reason for himself. Sometimes Dorone talks to him this way, but at least Dorone gets it; he hears it when Amur points it out.

"Tell me how you met." Orrus demands. He listens, rapt with attention, eyes bugging as though Amur's telling a wild tale. "He walked, on his own two feet, to your apartment? This is, I assume, not a *normal* event, an elderim come calling. I mean, it's been some time since I saw the Continent, of course, but… Well, you must have been shocked."

Shocked isn't the word, but Amur gives no more.

"How'd he *find* you?"

Amur looks to Dorone. "You tell it."

Dorone grins even though Amur isn't smiling. Two months in Iswee is a lot of parties, a lot of meeting people and being seen. He's heard Dorone tell the story—in grandiose mountaintop chateaus, in enchanted Elder cities whose names he can't pronounce, once on a floating island poised on the edge of a kilometer-high waterfall. Oh, he's heard it.

"I toured the university. You should've seen the campus, Orrus; it's quite lovely, actually. It feels old but I can't even recall how old. Desert air, desert sky, but lots of flowering trees and simple elegant buildings. The perfect place to meet Amur. I saw him and my heart—I tell you, my heart—well, my heart and maybe one other organ—felt simply *pulled* toward him. That body, that hair, that skin! Well, you see for yourself. And when I heard his *voice*, oh, the way I felt it vibrate in me..."

Amur isn't listening except to be annoyed by it. He wonders how he can feel so full of love, so full of lust, for this elderim prince when the guy can be so rote, so everyday, so basic. Not all the time. Around *them*.

"And so I asked the tour guide, *Do you know that one?* I pointed, I think. I must've looked like a fool, like I have no idea how to behave like an adult. She did, the guide—*Everyone knows this boy*, she said, with that exact tone. I asked where he lived. I *paid* her."

Orrus laughs. "You *paid* her?"

"Yes!" Dorone gives Amur a knowing glance. *You ok?* he mouths.

Finally, the elderim notices! Amur nods.

"He is the loveliest color, isn't he?" Dorone says. He grabs Amur's hand and squeezes. "Makes me wonder what other types of boys they're hiding from us in Jalast." He misinterprets Amur's expression. "It was a *joke*, love!"

"Your parents," Orrus presses. "They were educated in Nos Min?"

Amur nods, fighting the urge to comment on that word. *Educated.* First of his family to receive formal instruction past secondary school—and that in art, at the university. Unheard of. He stands taller as he walks. He inhales deeply, until his chest is filled with air and salt. At once, he recalls the joint folded in the waistband of his wrap. If he can get away.

"And your teachers? They were educated in Nos Min?"

Amur thinks about it—the joint, Orrus's question, the joint. Fuck it, what does it matter? He stops, gets the joint out, and turns to Dorone, who smiles his lovely lopsided smile and clicks his armored fingers, producing an amethyst flame above his palm. Amur takes a deep drag, gazes out at the ocean and back at his lover before looking the other elderim in the eye.

"I think so. Sure."

Orrus raises an eyebrow at Dorone. "What do you think *those* history lessons look like?" He returns his attention to Amur. "Eleven days! Tell me what you've seen of Iswee. What are your thoughts about our world—about us? Are you one of the restive ones we hear so much about, bent on our destruction? Of course, does it seem *right*, that we have so much and men have so little? But you know there are people starving on the Continent? Mismanagement!"

Dorone frowns. "No politics, Orrus."

Orrus laughs and slaps Amur's back. "It's good to smell the ocean again! It's been *weeks*." He whistles the way elderim do, so melodiously, and the Hound comes up, tongue out, looking so joyful. Amur looks away.

They keep walking. Amur fumes. Fucking elderim and their talking, their affection. Several times he convinces himself that he'll say something. He'll be the man and put it right out in the open. How far away is this fucking place of Dorone's, anyway?

He doesn't speak, though, and it's probably not that long a walk.

•

They round a sharp curve in the coastline. Beyond the bluff is a broad semicircular bay; Dorone points to the larger of two islands at its center, a couple kilometers offshore. He stretches his arms wide and grins, teeth and gums showing like a child.

"I have a home there, a small place. It's been some time. Problem with owning so goddamn many." He pulls Amur in close and grips his ass. Amur forces a smile and a laugh. Dorone calls to Orrus, "It's a short swim. What do you say?"

Orrus cocks an eyebrow. "A race, then? What about you, Amur? Judging by those shoulders, you'll be tough to beat."

Amur's temper flares. *Keep talking about my body, ancient.* He closes his eyes, remembers his breathing. He disengages from Dorone and lets his wrap fall to the ground. He stretches his long shapely limbs. He forces himself to move slowly, actual stretches instead of posturing, pretending to get ready. Both elderim stare at him. Of course they do.

Finished, he looks Orrus in the eye.

"How much of a head start do you need?"

A week before their departure, Amur announced that he'd be gone for the day. Dorone pouted and Amur was conflicted. Bringing the prince of the elderim home was a non-starter: "No, you can't come, Dorone; I get how charming you are and that makes no fucking difference." At the same time, leaving him in the apartment made Amur uncomfortable. He didn't want Dorone to be on his own. He wasn't in any danger; that was preposterous; but he'd wander around, coming and going from the building, drawing even more attention to himself, to Amur. Already, his friends were bugging him nonstop. He stopped going to classes that week because of it.

His mothers knew by now. Of course they did. He hadn't been home in nearly three months, but he'd been contracted to Dorone for two weeks and it was hopelessly public after the first few days. Jalast was nowhere important, but it wasn't that far.

That he was leaving with Dorone for Iswee: this would be new information.

The fifty-kilometer pedal from the capitol cleared his head. He didn't mind the wind in his face; the sky was cloudless and it went on forever; the air was filled with the smell of blooming cactus. He knew his strength and thrilled in it, grinning with the effort, snot flowing from his nose as he climbed the crumbling pavement of the switchbacks into the red hills, up onto the mesa. By the time he crossed under the cottonwoods into old town, he was good and tired and ready. He was known here, through and through: the lovely white-haird boy Amur (*oh, swoon*) had won every footrace, every wrestling match, nearly every goddamn *game*, since he was old enough to understand the difference between winning and losing. People stared as he pedaled past. People he'd known his entire life wore awed but unfriendly faces. A few punk girls spat near his feet, but he ignored them.

He kept his head up because, he reminded himself again, he'd *won* all those races. It wasn't even a contest, usually. Now he was at university, in the capitol, studying something special. He told himself he'd win at this, too, whatever mad thing it was that he was doing.

Mother Chora answered his clap at the door. She wore a new blue dress he liked. She didn't buy many new things, but with all but one kid out of the place maybe Okin was letting up a bit… She looked so lovely, her hips so grabbable in that dress, and he started to cry, but she gave him a look filled with the kind of disappointment he had nightmares about. She didn't hug him; nor did she invite him in. For the better part of an hour, he stood at the open doorway as she prepped dinner. He said nothing because it would've done no good.

Only when Agra arrived from work was he allowed in. He burst into tears at the sight of her. *Vedas*, she was radiant even in her drab secondary school pants. Alone in the family, she was as beautiful as him, as dark as him—she argued she was darker:

Oh, Amur, nope, look at how you're just the teensiest bit lighter around your palms. Not pure dark like me. I'm midnight, *kid.*

She took in his attire and whispered, *"Hoooooo,* boy." She'd always loved clothes, even more than he did; if she had her way she'd apprentice with a dyer or a clothier. Slimmer chance of that after Amur chose the university. Of course it pissed her off, and of course she got it like he got it. Nothing worked out, exactly, not in this family.

"I'm not even gonna start talking because, brother, I'll fuck you up," she said. "You're a fool. That's a kind word, woman. I mean, I'm in disbelief at your latest thing. And, but *no*, seriously, you *do not* understand how big a fucking deal this is. This is nothing like Marus. That was kid shit."

Now she looked like she was going to cry. It took a lot.

But she sighed and hugged him, placing her hand on the back of his head, stroking his hair like when she was tiny and he was only small. Her back was hard with muscle now. She was nearly as strong as him and a good deal faster, which was quite fast. That she wasn't quite as renowned pissed her off. *Just cuzza your hair, dummy*, she'd say.

He buried his nose in the fire-scented nest of her blueblack hair, which she kept fashionably untidy. His eyes filled again; he pushed her back, held her at arm's length. He didn't wipe the tears from his eyes, and she ran a fingertip along the hem of his sleeve.

He was smart enough not to talk sometimes, but only with her.

She didn't want to look at him but she also wanted to look at his clothes. His shirt and pants were of undyed cotton, but they were finer than anything she'd ever own. A gift from Dorone, of course. He watched her eyes. He pulled shirt and pants off and stood there in his pink briefs and nothing else. He held the clothes out to her. She shook her head, then took it. That he would go all the way back to Danoor in his underwear didn't alarm her. He never liked being covered up, though it had little to do with seeking attention.

"Eat," Chora said, dropping a bowl of bambooed rice and lamb on the kitchen counter. She looked at his near nakedness and frowned.

Amur shook his head. "Mom, it's not dinner t—"

"Don't care," she said. "I won't eat with a woman like you, not even sure you're my son anymore, but you've been let in here by someone and so I'll be damned if you leave without food in your belly. Stupid boy. You're too thin, Amur. Vedas, I'm always fucking telling you this."

She left the kitchen and stood next to Agra. They examined the clothes Amur gave her. He worried Chora would force Agra to give it back. But Chora whispered, *Hide it—hide it good.* Amur couldn't hear her whisper, but he was good at lip reading. The only boy had to be if he wanted to know what was going on.

He ate standing at the counter. His eyes roved around the small kitchen. The scarred, hand-and-knife-worn surfaces. There were darker areas on the tile floor, from lifetimes of bare feet passing over it, standing on it. So many small details he'd never noticed. He set his bowl down, unsure if he should wash it. He stood, rooted to the spot. Somewhere, probably in his mothers' bedroom, a radio was on, playing racha. Oldies.

The front door opened and closed. Mother Okin, returned for lunch. She took one look in the kitchen and turned away.

"Table," Chora called a moment later.

He and his mothers sat in the small dining room where they rarely ever ate. Agra stood in the doorway. Amur regarded Okin; he made himself stare her in the eye. Her heavy, tattooed arms. Her greying, matted locks. One eye was so dark it appeared black; the other was a milky orb, the result of an accident in youth. She'd never been a handsome woman, but she was interesting to look at. He hadn't ever liked her, and he no longer loved her because he knew better. But she was his mother. He'd drawn her many times.

She appraised her only son expressionlessly. "Let me see," she said, holding forth her large stonecutter hands. He placed his hands in hers. After a short examination, she grunted and let them go. "Not even *clay* under your nails. What do they have you doing in rich women land? It certainly isn't *work*." She sat back, chair groaning under her weight. "Why are you here, boy?"

He swallowed. "A blessing before I depart."

His mothers exchanged looks. Chora's mask went up over her fear. Old habit.

"Depart?" Okin said. "You already left."

His fists tightened in his lap. He took two long breaths. "I didn't. I went to school, to be the thing I've chosen to be."

Okin barked a laugh. "If you need to go there to be it, then it's a useless thing to be." She smiled and angled her head in a way he hated, like she was just a happy girl now. "But that's not why you're here, is it, elf-fucker?"

He closed his eyes. "You know he's chosen me, and that I've accepted. It is an honor, among some, to contract with an elderim this way, and I don't think all those men are all fools. Many of them are even vainer than me, but some are seeking something else from these people, as I'm seeking. I am seeking."

He swallowed and pressed on like always did in these moments, as if rehearsed rational thinking was any kind of thinking at all for his mothers. They hated him. No, just Okin. Chora loved him and wouldn't ever stop. She didn't understand him right now, and she was scared, and he understood. He spoke to her even though there was danger in that. He tried to be the son, her only son, the boy who charmed her so much with all his wanting pretty things and being such a good storyteller. She was a good mom even though she never had time, *she never had time.*

"This elderim is beautiful, mom, and I think I might love him for a while and it's been so long since I felt that way, and mine is a great honor, because of who Dorone is. This is like history happening, and I'll see so much. I understand your disappointment."

Okin's expression was now one of wonder. Oh, how her son speaks! He looked away from her and kept on.

"I don't know how long it'll last, the contract, but I'm being paid. A lot. And he's promised to show me how Iswee is changing, how they're rethinking their relationships here. Making things right. Reparations. Here, mom, listen; he says—"

He stopped because Okin was looking at Chora, who'd begun to tremble.

"Why are you talking to *her*?" Okin said.

Chora closed her eyes. Okin's expression was intent; she appeared not to breathe. Agra left her spot. The front door opened and slammed.

"I'm being paid," Amur repeated. A stupid thing to say that would make no difference—he'd seen a hundred arguments; had Okin ever bent? Give her all the money in the world. Nothing would change her mind and he was an absolute idiot to think it would be otherwise. Regardless. "A huge amount, more than our family could earn in lifetimes. Like an elderim, an Isweean. No man's been contracted as Dorone's consort in decades; do you know what that means? I can help us, the family. I can pay off Herena's debt; I can repair gramma's well, *like that*. A few months, maybe a year, is all. You wouldn't have to work ever again."

Okin leaned forward and rested her arms on the table. Slowly, she raised her hands and steepled her fingers, displaying the scrollwork script tattooed from elbow to wrist, a line of classical Nosi mirrored on each arm. *Loyal to Blood. Loyal to Blood.* Proof that you stand with Jalast, the first people of the mesas, that you live the ways of old Nosi and refuse any state assistance from the elderim. But for a trip to the eastern border with Toma as a child and the rare trip to the capitol, Okin rarely set foot outside Jalast.

"You'll get no blessing here," she said. "You're not my son."

Insubordinately, Amur looked to Chora. Sensing his gaze, she opened her eyes.

Okin snapped her fingers in Amur's face. "Don't look at *her*. She's not your mother, either. Find your father if you're hungry for approval." She closed one fist and inserted her index finger into it, pumping in and out. *"Men* are all you ever cared about, anyway."

Amur stood, waiting for permission to leave. Okin stared at him, eyebrows raised. Chora stared at the table. He turned and walked out of the house. He passed the mens commons where his father lived but didn't inquire after him. The man would cry and plead with Amur, who would leave drunk, lightened of half his coin. His father was better at pretending, now that Amur had money from the scholarships. Amur fell for it a few times. That feeling they understood one another, followed by the realization, when he sobered, that he'd lost something in the exchange. His father never really *listened*, did he?

He said no goodbyes as he walked out of Jalast.

The island is sparsely wooded with scraggly irel pine on the northern side. The house sits back from the southern shore, on a small bluff of weathered blue stone overlooking the open sea. There are no other structures; there is no source of freshwater. It's lovely, Amur notes, but not remarkably so. The home, likewise, is uninspiring, white-stuccoed like those in Kua but smaller than the homes there, more modest. Unlike the royal family's households elsewhere—the sprawling, multilevel apartments and vast estates overlooking every kind of shore and valley and mountain in Iswee—this home appears built for one, perhaps two.

Three years ago, Mother Okin and Grandfather Acher built not half such a home for Nelada and her new wife. Nel was the second oldest and least tethered to reality of his sisters; she'd envisioned something much grander.

Dorone grips the door handle and pauses, grinning back at Amur. "I used to come here after months-long campaigns on the Continent—after the war, diplomacy mostly, which is even more tiring than war. I'd spend a few nights here, to get my mind right. Better to address Council and King with a few night's peace behind you; of course, it pisses them off to be kept waiting…"

The Hound barks at the house. She follows closely behind Orrus but stops before crossing the threshold. She stands stiff-legged and growling, hackles up, snuffling smoke as the screen door closes in her face. Orrus lets the door close behind him, but turns back to her. He crouches with the screen door separating them. He orders her to sit.

"It's okay, baby. I'm just in here." He presses his hand to the screen. She sniffs it, and licks the bamboo lattice. Orrus says something too soft for Amur to hear.

Amur watches, filled with an awful emotion.

("It's the salt on my hands," Marus says, staring up at him. The dog next to him, mouth open, smiling wide.)

"Coffee?" Dorone says. "I haven't been here in a few years, but the place was cleaned and stocked for our arrival." He opens and closes a few cabinets. "Ah! Only take a moment."

Amur looks around the place. Solid pine construction with no plaster ornamentation but plenty of windows. One main room, a kitchen, a study, a bedroom, and a bathroom—each populated with comfortable but worn furniture and an enviable variety of canvases on the walls. Unlike elsewhere in Iswee, there are none of the usual elderim conveniences: no lamps you can turn on with a word, no hot or cold air you can summon from vents using a slightly different word. When night falls, the house will be lit by electric lamps, like in Amur's home.

It's difficult to imagine Dorone spending time here.

"Different from what I expected," he says. "In a good way. I like it, Dorone."

Dorone chuckles. He runs his fingers through his hair, gazing out the window. "Sure, I understand that. It is different, I agree. I should come here more often, to remember what it's like to live this way. Come, *sit sit.*"

They sip coffee. Dorone fills in the growing silences. Orrus's eyes rove the interior of the cabin, lingering here and there. He stares for a length of time at a crystal globe positioned on a stand before two glass-paneled doors leading out back. Sunlight scatters through the globe, throwing a spectrumed ball of light on the floor. What does he see in the ceiling beams, the knife-scratched kitchen counter, the table's chipped wood grain? What of that painting, of the mother and child picnicking together? This is Dorone's home, but Orrus knows it well.

Amur doesn't say anything. He's again thinking about Marus, and Marus's dog. He doesn't want to think about it, not here, not anywhere. But *here* is particularly bad. He shouldn't have smoked the whole joint.

Orrus stands, pours himself more coffee. The Hound raises her head to stare inside. She gets up and circles twice, whining.

"Shush, baby," Orrus says. "Shush down. We're just talking."

Dorone smiles. "Not long now, Orrus. Come, finish your coffee."

Amur stares at his hands, holding the mug. He fiddles with the mug.

The slide of a chair. Orrus sits. After a long pause, he sighs.

"I have to use the bathroom," Amur says, too loudly.

Idiot. He's an idiot and a coward. He shuts the door and leans, backside against the sink, staring at the painted floor tiles. He turns to the basin as a wave of nausea passes through him. Acid rises into his mouth with a burp. He spits into the sink and then listens. Dorone and Orrus aren't speaking. Amur pulls the chain and returns to the table. Neither elderim has moved. Their mugs sit untouched before them.

Dorone pushes his chair back and stands. Amur's heart pounds.

"Right," Orrus says. "This thing." He slaps his hand on the table. Amur flinches and the mugs jump. The Hound gets up and barks. "Nine hundred *years*, Dorone. My father won't stand for it, nor will my uncles and brothers. You're going to start a war, a civil war, and for what?" He gestures to Amur. "Is this one somehow more special than past ones? You've run out of romantic shit to do and so you do this to me, now? You don't *need* her, Dorone."

"I'm not starting a war. I'm righting a wr—"

Orrus smacks the table again. The *crack* of the wood giving way. The elderim stares at the fracture line under his fist. He lifts his hand to stare at what he's done. For a moment he looks like he'll cry, and Amur wants to look away but doesn't. He won't move.

"So, we're doing *that*, then," Orrus says, voice flat. "You're bored again, looking for projects—*symbols*. You and your fucking *drama*. How'd it work out last time you gave them *hope* like this? Patterns of bullshit." He gestures at Amur. "How far did you have to look to find one stupid enough to believe all this? Playing games with *children*, Dorone! I still remember that one, name begins with a B—did you wash those sheets or just throw them out?"

"Don't," Dorone says.

Orrus angles his head up and spits expertly. The gob hits Dorone square in the chest.

Dorone leans forward, resting his fists on the table, one lavender, the other the deep blues of a dusk sky. Amur watches the line where the armor stops on Dorone's bicep. He expects the line to break now, for the armor to spread onto Dorone's body in anticipation of violence. They've talked a lot about violence, he and Dorone. Stories.

"You're forgiven," Dorone says. "I know you care for it. Her. What do you want—to see if she'll fight me?" He waits a moment, brows raised, then straightens. Hands on hips, he stretches for show. "It'll get ugly, that way." He walks to the door. "This is what's best, Orrus."

The front door clicks shut behind Dorone, obscuring the beach beyond. The slap of the screen door follows, ringing.

Judror, Kingdom of Casta Setjis
(Summer—26 years old)

He keeps Sroma's soul in a heavy locket on a catgut cord around his neck. He opens the locket rarely, and only for himself. If a guy stays over, he sleeps with it clenched in his fist over his heart. He can let other things go.

"So what is that? Looks expensive. Lucky marble? Pic of your mum?"

"Drugs is what it is, right?"

He's never been good at honesty, and this is an easy lie. "Nah. Nothing—it's empty. I picked it up in Horsteads. I do like it, though; it was the first pretty thing I bought when I moved here. I should put something in it."

It isn't actually a pretty pendant, and he's never a good liar for long. He can't part with the thing. After a while, if he lets a guy stick around long enough, it becomes a source of contention. Confusion turns to suspicion, to irritation; he can't hide how important it is to him and he refuses to explain it.

There are other things, of course, like *where's your family* and *how have you got so much money*. Other things can be avoided. Not hidden—avoided.

And so, eventually, no matter how good it *can* be it ends in a mess.

"What so important could fit in something so small?"

"Why's it matter so fucking much? I'm sure you just left it at your place."

"You say it's empty. You're a liar, like a real crazy person. It shouldn't be this big a thing, this or any of the other weird shit you can't talk about. Just tell me what's going on in your *brain*, Amur."

He can run or swim or bike and lose himself in it. He can relax in his studio even though his body's as tense as a bowstring; he's got time to stare at the paper, consider each deliberate step if deliberate is how he's going. He's always drawn in pen. He likes the feel of a near disaster— the way you can't back out once you've put a line down.

In a fight, you're just as committed, but you can't relax. You're always focused on this creature set against you.

Sometimes it's only exhausting. No rush, no sense of accomplishment. On days like today, when the sun stays locked behind a ceiling of clouds and it just mists all the damn time, when he stays cooped up in his apartment in lieu of visiting his studio, he's sluggish and the matches are grueling in a way he resents—his body should move better than this. He's more likely to get hurt but he does it anyway.

He walks to the less preferred gym, which is farther away but never has any lavenders. He has no patience for that shit right now. Halfway there, the rain starts up. Should've ridden his bike. He picks up the pace, chin on his chest, warm rain running down his back, cyclists in the slow lane kicking up puddles onto his feet. Three years. He's never going to get used to it; there's never *not* water in the air.

He manages a clumsy hour of wrestling and boxing and leaves after dark, sore in body and restive of mind. Cut above the right eye, purple lump of a bruise on his right thigh, causing him to list; he thinks grumpy thoughts as the rain resumes. Under the awning of a kabob shop, he eats fast food slowly, thinking of places he might go, people he might see. He's lonely. There are bars, where there are people, close by. He may strike up a conversation. He walks himself through the steps. It's just too much work.

"You and me," he says to Sroma.

Alone in the Docksides apartment that smells of unwashed sweaty clothes, he takes a quick and completely inadequate shower, unwraps a lemon pastry, and smokes a bowl. It's humid as hell because there's no goddamn wind and his hair is a fucking disgusting mess; he scratches at his scalp, feeling the sebum gathering under his fingernails, which also need a trim. He turns the ceiling fan on high, sets the floor fan up. He draws for a while, then puts all the lights out except one small alchymical lamp with its constant amber glow. He leans against the street-facing wall, listening to a couple guys talking loudly on the street three storeys down.

"...and that's *why* it's bullshit." Local guy. "No, I'm *not* trying to start a fight here. I'm *not*, I promise mate. It's just you say we have to work with them. Over and over again you say this, I get so tired of hearing it. And all *I'm* saying is they can't be worked with. You know this, how I feel, why're we talking about it even one more time?"

"Nah, nah! I mean, yeah, we talk about it to death. We *do*. Remember that time at Ansell's. We *ruined* that party." He laughs good and hard. "But you still, no I'm serious, you *still* never answer me: how's it all gonna change that way, that extreme. *We're not stronger than them*. This is like the fundamental problem right here, all the time, with *everybody*. What, *you're* so tough all of the sudden?"

Amur can't place the second man's accent. He listens for a bit but neither the accent nor their argument becomes much clearer to him. He's not paying real close attention, because all you need are a few words and how they're said to know. He suspects which side they're on, of course, otherwise he wouldn't still be listening, and the guys move on to other shit—complaints, mostly, though they laugh a lot, like they know each other well. Amur listens, enjoying the sound of the words and sometimes the words themselves. Local guy impersonates his wife, and it's clear he respects her, which makes Amur smile.

They laugh. "Gotta go," odd accent says. "*Be with you.*"

Amur closes his eyes, nods his head: good men. And then he's angry, that quickly, because he's been reminded of *them*, of *him*. He's reminded a lot, so it's nothing to get upset about. He breathes in and fills his belly, his whole body, and forgets about it.

He closes his shutters against his neighbors. He puts on a record, something muddy and distorted and *lovely*—Truce's *An Olive Branch On The Bed, Pictures Of Vedas And Military Clothes*. He kneels, lifts the catgut over his head, and places the locket face up in his palm. As always, it feels heavier in his hand than he imagined, and the metal is warmer than it should be, even after resting upon his chest all day. Most of the time he thinks of Sroma as happy and warm in there, cuddled into a ball, dreaming. Sometimes she's raging, twisting against the walls of her prison, forever howling flame. He imagines opening the locket, smashing the marble against the floor, watching her soul rise as fire, eating through the ceiling and into the sky. He follows, lifting free of the floor, hurling his body over the rooftops of Judror, over the Continent entire and across the sea, returning to Iswee, soaring over it until he comes to the beach on the island where Dorone's house stands. Orrus's house. He sets his feet upon the shore. Here, the hundred rulers of Iswee have gathered. Chin high, he surveys them in their Elder relics, their glorious rainbow-hued armor. They stand as motionless as statues, as sharp as blades. He's jealous of them, but he's also proud of his pure black nudity, his blindingly white halo of hair, his perfect simplicity.

:Where is he?: he asks the popinjays.

They part from before Dorone's house, revealing his enemy encased in the jeweled aspect of his armor.

No words are satisfying to imagine at this juncture—everything he or Dorone may say just gets in the way, ruining his anger—so he doesn't speak before or after breaking every bone in Dorone's body. He executes the prince before his people, bending Dorone's glorious body over his knee, severing the elderim's spine with a loud crack.

And then he rockets off, into the sky, to anywhere. Gone away, like Vedas.

Sometimes, he does open the locket. Sometimes, he holds Sroma's soul in his hands. It glows faintly against the creases of his palms, pulsing like a heartbeat. He presses his face close, until red light fills his vision. He focuses on it, light and rhythm, until his eyes water and his neck grows sore from the posture. Until the red becomes black, and his head swims. As if she'll tell him something, reveal the sense in his choices.

Tonight, he returns the locket to its place resting between the muscles of his chest. The tension in his shoulders has loosened; he stretches like a cat, holding the postures until balance seems impossible and he tumbles to the floor. For a while, he loses track of his place in the world and simply stands in the center of his apartment, hips swaying to an unheard beat. That restless cycle of thought winds down, quieting to a whisper.

"I try to leave, I try to leave, I try to leave," he talk-sings. The song dredges up something he doesn't want to think about right now, so he stops. It's cool; he's got lots of other songs in his head, though fewer new ones lately. He needs to get a life.

His hand descends. Sex. Always the most reliable option,

and he doesn't even bother trying other fantasies: he imagines Dorone tensed above him, his face in ecstasy. The elegant lines of his body, the sounds he made. His ears, his ass. Amur moans and disrobes and lays on the floor, grimacing at the dirt and crumbs under his back. Fingertip pressed against his asshole, fist pumping on his cock, the orgasm is quick and satisfying. He just spreads the cum around on his chest, letting it dry sticky. He tips his head to each side without the usual resistance, and gets the tumbling pop of vertebrae so satisfyingly it makes him shiver.

He sits up and surveys the rumpled mess of dirty bed sheets, the crusty pile of dishes next to the sink—the open boxes of pigments and paints, scattered and cracked and useless now. He whispers He turns all the lights on. In the sudden brightness, his digs are even worse. Feeling that rare burst of energy, like a gift, he gets to work.

Eventually, he tries to go to sleep and can't. He smokes some more and makes it worse. He thinks about the future, the thing that scares him the most—because why not, yeah? He's always been good at putting his mind through hell.

He thinks how it won't always be this way, that one day he'll grow close enough to someone, he'll actually prefer someone's company *enough*, to talk of things that might occur in a week, a month, a year. How he'll feel happy and maybe they'll talk about *family* and what that will mean, together. He thinks about how he'll fuck that all up. Because he won't discuss where the money came from and he won't really talk about his family. And the locket. Of course the fucking locket.

Having fucked it up, he'll do what he does already but without the good part—the hope will eventually up and leave him. He'll lose partners, turn away from friends. No family, as if such a thing needs stating. And so much wealth, not spent in excess or to help others but trickled out, uselessly, boringly. He'll come to dress in pants and blouse like everyone else here. (There are other places he's been! Places he liked *more*, actually, filled with color and light! A boy caused it. A boy always causes it. He stayed after the breakup because it's easier to stay.) He'll eat too much at the same restaurants. He'll drink to excess and be, now and then, poetic in his drunkenness. He'll create art that mimics itself, exacter and exacter copies of what he thought was good when he was young, like he can't fucking *grow* anymore. He'll move from apartment to apartment in the same familiar wet sock of a city, circling around the Isweean Consulate at its center as though Dorone will alight upon its multi-domed roof and offer him something more.

He wakes before fully rested and goes about his routine—meals at these times; a run around the Keers at noon when everyone else is locked inside, away from the heat; followed by the three-kilometer bike ride to his studio overlooking the Aurumel River Locks, where he smokes dope, drinks plum wine, and chips away at the same self-study he's been working on for five months, before ending it at Shem's, sweating a body length from other young men and women in the ring.

There are more efficient places to hone one's skill; in the clubs that hunch over the Yan River a fighter can truly measure themself. But Amur knows enough fighters with missing teeth, sooky eyeballs, permanently gimped legs, and worse, all because they fought when exhaustion or age told them they should keep seated. Amur can afford to make it a lifestyle, training at the manicured gyms near the city center.

He's been to the clubs. He's done well. But he won't press it. When they see how pretty he is, how *rare*, they get weird. Some want to hurt him, just looking at him.

Exercises over, a good-looking redhead walks over. They've exchanged words before, but Amur can't recall his name. The intent is clear, and the other man knows Amur knows it.

"Wanna get a drink?" the man says. What a line.

Amur balks. He rarely dates fighters; the industry appeals to a certain sort, the kind who waste their off time drinking and starting fights at football matches. The more *purpley* sort. Today, he counted three lavender-shell anklets. He didn't pull his punches against them, and he often pulls his punches. This dude's clear.

"I'd love to, some other time," he says. He smiles, picturing Agra so it's a real smile. His best trick. "I work early tomorrow."

The redhead shrugs like it's nothing, but Amur recognizes his disappointment. He's been caught out in a lie, too; people with *jobs* don't train here four nights a week. (They also don't have bodies, or skin, or hair, like Amur does. That takes lots of pampering and rest.) He stares at the redhead's chest, struck by the healthy glow of his pale skin, the quick pulse at the base of his neck.

Amur reconsiders; this tiredness doesn't *have* to last, does it? He's not required to live his life this way, saying no before he's even thought it through.

"Some other time, sure," the redhead says.

Amur watches the play of muscle in the man's back, and wonders if the moment can be salvaged. But the guy's already made his way across the gym and Amur shudders at the idea of interrupting his conversation, explaining how he's such a fool—some lie about forgetting his schedule and of course he can have a drink. Or something. He'll mangle it if he tries. It'll still *work*, though.

He steps out and hails a pedicab across downtown, in search of somewhere new to eat. He pays little mind to the sights—canal boats passing under bridges, bands playing mostly shitty music in bars, cafes spilling young pretty people into the evening. There are even a few elderim around, surrounded by the beautiful, clueless boys they've purchased for the evening. Other, tougher-looking men hover at the edges of these groups, trying to look normal and failing. Bodyguards. As if one elderim alone couldn't handle some men. As if men aren't generally smarter than that. Just *touching* one of them will get you killed, mate. Best not even think in their direction.

It's an exaggeration, but not so far off.

He used to be unable to look away from them. It made him so goddamn anxious, this obligation he had to always look. Now he just fucking hates them and that's that.

"You know a good place to eat, maybe a good beer, round here?" he asks the cabbie, and winces; that's one of the dumbest sentences he's ever said. Like he's hitting on her. She's gorgeous, he'll admit, lithe and broad shouldered in fringed buckskin shorts and a kaleidoscopic breast wrap. Her legs are envy-inducing. She turns her head; a sharp profile underscored by the angular spikes of her straw-colored hair. He guesses that she listens to pretty good music, or at least not bar music.

"Gotta be honest, mate, not my scene!" She turns further to see him and keeps pedaling. He grips the cushion underneath him and suffers the shame of not being cool.

You chose to live here, man.

She shouts. "I dig your hair. Where you from?"

He smiles. Sometimes that kind of compliment pisses him off, but not usually when it comes from people younger than him. "Nos Min. I came here three years ago."

Her head is turned forward again. "Whoa! Way far, mate!"

He tips her well (he tips everyone well) and surveys his options. He visits the Assembly Quarter rarely. More elderim live here. At least in his neighborhood, tall buildings block his view of the consulate, but here it's ever present, its grey elderstone walls rising above the shops and brownstone rowhouses. The complex beyond the wall is massive, occupying what used to be the original city square.

"They paid for it," a woman once told him. A stranger who saw him staring.

"What?" he said.

"The property, the ground," the woman said, pointing to the consulate. "They *paid* us for it."

He stares at the walls now, imagining a city square instead. He walks, inevitably, until he's before the consulate wall. He presses his hand to the stone, marbled with blue and yellow strands and polished to a high sheen. The silver mortar between each meter-squared block is perfect, no variance in thickness or application.

"Fucking ugly," he says. No, not ugly—just infuriating. The Continent's only source of elderstone is Noerre, a mine west of Jalast on the flank of the mesa. Prior to the treaty of Dombur, Amur's ancestors refined dust from the elderstone, using it to make bombs and cannon powder. For generations, they kept Noerre from falling into enemy hands.

He wonders how much the elderim paid for this show of opulence, this insult to his people. He thinks of Okin, how enraged she'd be seeing it. *What, the elves don't have enough of their own fucking godrock to build with?*

Someone has tagged one of the lower blocks.

WeeanGOTTAgo it reads in a scrawling, multicolored script. Below it, a smaller tag by the same hand: *v-e-d-a-5-b-e-w-i-t-h-m-e*

Amur grins and runs his finger over the words; some sort of wax pen, easy to wash off. It'll be scrubbed by tomorrow. A neighbor will see it and fear retribution, a boycott of their bakery or watch repair. Policing their own people on the elderim's behalf, and it pisses him off but he understands. People need to make a living, provide for their families. They don't want it to escalate.

A cop walks up the avenue. He smiles at her and she frowns. He moves along.

He eats at a tightly packed Serenali barbecue. People gather in a circle around the spinning grill, spearing the choicest bits of pork belly and squid before they pass. Glasses raised; hugging all around; he drinks with them and understands at some point that he has joined a wedding anniversary celebration. Everybody silly, everybody paired up. He thinks of the redhead. Would've been so much easier. He buys a swarthy Serenali man a drink but the man smiles and nods at the man next to him. *Sorry*, the man mouths. Two of the women have lavender-colored hoops in their ears. Amur returns home, fuller and drunker than he intended.

Music sounds nice, but he can't think of anything to listen to. He stares at the waxpaper box in his hands. An older woman, drunk and aggressively flirtatious but with no ill intent, made him take it home with him. He unwraps it and sits in his favorite new armchair with the food in his lap, mind empty as he picks out the slightly burnt bits. The overhead fan does nothing. *Vedas*, he feels greasy, Before long, the food is gone and he slumps further into the soft leather cushions with one shapely leg thrown over the armrest. He angles his head to look out the unshuttered eastern window, spotting Berun but not Fyra. The little moon looks stuck in the starry sky, but if Amur waits long enough it moves, closer and closer to the edge of the frame. A breeze winds through the apartment, making the sketches in an open folio before him shudder. A picture of a boy and a dog. Amur closes the folio. He tugs at the locket, pulling the catgut tight across the back of his neck as two people begin arguing in the street below.

Prota, Medile Sea
(Spring—46 years old—2 years old)

Once a month, he pedals twelve kilometers inland to Etche—to check the post, pay the electricity bill, and run errands. His post box is typically empty, though occasionally he receives a book or record after months of waiting. He buys spices, canned goods, and beer. Sometimes he buys tackle or hunting supplies (arrows, typically, which he'll only lose; he's better with the sling). He doesn't mind the errands, and saves his visit with Dansia for last. He likes hearing about the world, hearing it from her mouth.

He misses Sroma. He worries too much about her.

He wakes as normal and takes her for a run. He offers her a quick violent wrestle that surprises and delights her, but when he shoulders his rucksack she knows what's up. She whines and makes those eyes at him. When he attaches the trailer to the bike, she howls.

"Oh, you're fine," he tells her, but it's hard to leave. He picks at the itchy scab on his forearm, peeling it back and watching the blood well under it, gummy and hardening already. She bit him hard, only a moment ago, burying all four canine teeth in him; if he pauses to watch long enough, the wound will heal completely. "You got more than enough yesterday. *And* just now. Vedas, that fucking stings."

She stays put because he tells her, and he sings her a childish tune—*she is a good girl, isn't she, isn't she?*, ad nauseum—long after he's out of earshot.

He pedals to Merit, where he whistles at the blind old Tomen and sets his tires upon the road to Etche. It's a climb the whole way, and the road is muddy from recent storms. Tall pines shadow the road more often than not, though; the air is cool and perfumed. He falls over twice in the mud, and sometimes he goes slower than a man walks, and he feels ridiculous and joyful. The dust sings like daylight in his veins, like it rarely does, and he misses her, and worries, he's always worrying, but it's okay for now. By the time he's close to the city, coasting down the mostly dry hardpack road into the valley, sometimes with both hands off the handlebars, he's spattered in dried mud and grinning.

Etche sits in the near-exact center of Prota, in a verdant valley enclosed by low hills to the north, south, and west, with the half-kilometer vertical face of Mt Adlean looming in the east. At its center is a small saltwater lake called Maoge. Founded by Ulome after Adrash's death and the calming of the sea, it seems to Amur like every other old Ulome city, spread out as far as the landscape will allow with a lot of space between its sturdy aracora-beamed houses and businesses. Its avenues are well plotted, with streetlights on every corner, even on the outskirts.

Isolated on their small island in the ass-end of nowhere, the population has turned provincial; he can't predict who'll be welcoming, who'll be standoffish. Their behavior often confuses him. He's never had much trouble with accents, but Protan is hard to follow.

Three blocks in and kids have already latched onto him. To ask questions, to hawk fruit and candy, or just to stare. "You're so *tall*! Why are you so tall? You're so *black*! Why're you so..." He smiles for them, pointing to his mouth and pantomiming muteness. They know he's lying but don't care because he's generous. He buys candy and gives the candy away. He lets them hang from his outstretched arms a few times before telling them to get lost and getting back on his bike. They laugh and follow for a bit. Adults, he generally tries to ignore. There's a fair bit of traffic at this hour, though, and Ulome walk and bike rapidly on their meticulously smooth roads. He has to communicate to navigate the streets.

They have nice legs in this place, he admits; he likes the way they hike the hems of their skirts up into their belts when they're pedaling. And the sun does them good; they're not as pale as their cousins on the Continent. They wear more color.

He gets a lot of looks, and a younger him might have looked back.

He runs his errands quickly but politely. He stops at a cafe bakery; he eats six small quiches and two glazed scones while he reads from the book he's brought—the rattier of two copies of his favorite novel, *Kirith Kirin*. He takes a nap on a bench in a park. Midafternoon, he heads to the city center, to Dansia's. As in all Ulome cities, there's a sharp line separating communally owned land from city founder's land; though permitted under law, most residents don't set foot in the city center. The closest they get to it is the ring of marketplaces that surround it—markets being the one place in an Ulome city where everyone is expected to mingle.

(Another Ulome city: A boy steps onto the marble paving stones to get his rubber ball. A patrolwoman steps from out of the marketplace and grabs the boy's wrist. She lifts the boy off his feet. With her other hand, she slaps the boy across the face. Again, and again.

"Hey!" Amur calls.

The patrolwoman looks over.

People *scram*; Amur stands by himself, gaze locked with her.)

"Otchelum," he whispers, surprised by the clarity of the memory. He hated that city. Did he leave it be with the patrolwoman, or did he get himself in trouble?

He walks around the northern half of the lake, peering into the shallow, glass-clear depths. Fed with seawater from deep fissures in the island's crust, the lake's current once stole two young torpaedo from the sea. Grown too large to escape, they now swim in an unending circle, their dull grey eyes forever angled to the upper boundaries of their confinement. They will live a thousand years.

Any moment, someone, some absolutely *draped* aristocrat will come with a sedated copperfin from the market. The copperfin is absurdly fast; when it hits the water it becomes a metallic red streak. But the long-snouted torpaedo are smarter; they hunt like men, coordinating their movements. On weekends, rich women sit along the lakeshore, betting on which torpaedo will snap up their copperfin.

He's allowed into the city center.. He's *rare*, like Dansia.

Her place sits a block back from the lakefront residences and shops. Dansiarra Ulasz, of Bonbur in central Nos Min, is the best brewer in the city. She's blunt, a dull blade—straightforward in a way that makes him feel at home. She reminds him of someone. He recalled who it was, once, maybe it was only last visit, but that memory is gone. One of his mothers, maybe one of his sisters. His father, he suspects, wasn't so frank.

He surprised himself on their first meeting, only his second day on the island. He just wanted to get to the cabin he'd bought, sight unseen. He just wanted to know that he was truly alone, where he could think and move without consideration of anyone else. He needed room to get over his fear of the dust, and fuck if he hadn't had enough of cities; they got between him and the clarity he sought. Why wait around this place and know any of these people?

He was disarmed by Dansia's charm, though—that and the way she didn't seem to think anything of his hair or his body. She looked at his ass, sure, but only the way a fan of good butts looks at another butt. He admired hers in turn. She was large and strong. He got drunk and stayed late.

"I don't drink anymore, actually," she told him before getting shitfaced alongside him. They talked of home—good things, and also deep wounds, and he felt bad lying to her about so much. His feelings weren't always a lie. She put on records, and it was good music, nothing like he ever listened to, all throbbing beats and hushed repetitive singing, like temple singing but weirder, uglier and prettier at once.

It was easy, imagining what life he could have had. He invented a family like his own, but better—in truth, he just remembered what good he could and said that. He didn't even invent a name for Agra because that seemed crass. He remembered her then, perfectly. He remembered Chora, and he might have kept her name the same, too. He didn't talk of violence and didn't need to. She could see it in the lines of his face. He was an angry, restive man, and he didn't try to hide it.

It would be the only time they talked so much of themselves. Maybe she lied as much as he did; she certainly kept major things out, as is anyone's right. He didn't know why she'd come here, and it didn't matter. It was good. She insisted he stay, sleep on the couch. She insisted, swore she'd rather die than have a cousin, no matter how distantly related, sleep in a *hotel bed* when she had a couch, a couch she *loved*, for him to occupy. He swore he'd stay.

She fell asleep at the table, drooling on her forearms. He carried her heavy body to her apartment upstairs and laid her in bed. He didn't know what to do after that; she might be sick, and he swore; so he stayed in her main room, reclining on her couch. Not sleeping.

A novel and oddly exhilarating feeling, being in a woman's place again. He recalled: there was this same smell in his sisters' rooms, a care taken *not* to stink. He touched nothing except a statuette on the table before him. A short-haired Churli, companion to Vedas, an ancient god of the Castans. Its surface was well worn, comfortable in his hand. A dulled, wonderful thing. The kid in him wanted it, wanted to take it. He'd often stolen pretty things, when he was young. He'd wanted things so badly when he was young.

Dansia roused just after daybreak and walked out to find him there. After blinking bleary eyes in his direction for a while, she said, "It's nice to wake up to *coffee*, cousin. I mean, it's right here on the fucking counter."

***

"Ah," she says as he stoops to enter the taproom. The place is dark, the shutters still closed. "Get out," she tells the other guy at the bar—the only guy in the place this early. The Ulome opens his mouth to object but shuts it when he registers the tall, half-naked man standing next to him. The Ulome's pale, doughy face is even uglier when it leers. Amur gives him a hard no look and the guy leaves.

"Dansia," Amur says. He grins, surprised by his own joy. "Good to see you."

"Same." She smiles, but there's nothing in it.

"What's going on?"

She rounds the bar and locks the door. She pulls two beers and they sit. He tastes his and compliments it. She nods, eyes tight and lips pinched in hard thought. He was raised right; he sits and waits. He watches her, though. He feels comfortable enough doing that, even now. He notices how many freckles she has on her cheeks—they're so close to her natural brown that he never noticed.

Maybe he did notice.

"There's a city in Zonir, near the Cousin," she says. Her voice is rough. She sips her beer, pauses, and shakes her head. "Graslea. Maybe five hundred women. Lots of artists. My wives and I went there, ten years after we wed. A honeymoon, I suppose, because we hadn't ever had one. Everyone was so busy, all the fucking kids everywhere. I was very young, though, still, only twenty-five, maybe twenty-six. I didn't know what I had. It sits in this canyon. Graslea. Probably the most beautiful place I've ever been. I wanted to live there." She gestures with her hands, like she's defining a wave. "The rocks are amazing. Were amazing. It's gone."

He sits with this for a second. "Gone?" he says, a foolish thing anyone will say. He leans forward. Under the table, his hands clasp together tightly enough to pulverize bone. His chest swells, quivering. "Destroyed."

She nods. "Yeah. *That.* I knew one woman there, though we haven't exchanged letters since I moved here. I assume he's gone now, too." She formed her lips around the word. *Destroyed.* "Happened two months ago, I heard yesterday, a letter from my aunt. No one here cares." She shrugs. "I don't talk to many people. But still. We're all women. We're not *them.*"

He waits. He hasn't heard her talk like she's in the desert in a while.

"A group of them were visiting. Tourists, of course, slumming. Someone, some woman, no name but I'm sure they'll find one—they threw a bomb right in the center of them. From a roof, my aunt says. An actual bomb, the kind we made way back when. I didn't know we could do that anymore. I'm not sure *they* knew."

She gets up, opens a box on the bar, and gets a cigarette. She raised her eyebrows and gestures to the counter. He declines.

"They came, within hours. Of course they did, Dorone and Anetter and the others whose names I used to fucking know. ... Why do we know them still? Seriously, *why*, why do we know them like they're footballers or something? Because they're charming liars. Because nothing ever gets better, not for most of us. It's always bullshit."

Her expression collapses. She covers her face with her hands. She wipes the snot from her nose with her hand. She stares at her hand.

"They melted the city into the ground. All of it, now a pool of glass at the bottom of a burnt canyon. They've begun looking in other cities, my aunt says. Of course they have. Women will disappear. It won't be the elderim who take them. My brother—" She swallows, closes her eyes, and breathes deep. "He organized a rally two years ago. They'll remember him. It might not be so bad. Maybe it'll be bad."

He stares at the tabletop.

"They've ruined us, you know? They're making us two different types of women. A rational one, and an idiot. That's the violence I'm talking about, cousin—do you understand, do you *see*? So what if it's been two hundred years since Dombur, if only every two hundred years they murder a whole fucking town? It's all the time, what they do to us!"

She looks away and smokes.

Amur nods, knowing and not knowing. What he knows is obvious, for all Nosi know it. He was born on the hundred and fiftieth anniversary of Dombur. His full name, Amureru: it means Retribution in Classical Nosi. Common name for generations.

What he doesn't know isn't about facts, or narratives. He's been away, he's been pretending, he's had money and freedom—too much for any man's good. He knows this. And it's not his choice, what the dust takes. He knows less each day.

Dansia's eyes are wet and red-rimmed; her hair, always so tidy, is coming out from her headwrap. Brass-black coils—he wants to reach across the table and tuck them in, or do a neat little braid. ("Look at me! You're better at this than your sister, little man." A kind voice, and he aches to hear it again. And then it's gone; he can't recall any of it, like it never happened.) He looks at her hands. They're large, strong, thick-skinned from decades of work. Slowly, deliberately, he takes her hands in his, a family sort of gesture. He can't look her in the eye.

"I feel it, Dansia."

"I know you do." She squeezes his hands then pulls them gently free. She waits until he meets her gaze. "Heartbreak, Amur," she says. She snubs her smoke and gets another. "Heartbreak *and* rage. Exhaustion. They loosen the tongue—you say things that have been on your mind a while. or it's an excuse and I'm just tired." She grabs his empty glass and leans over the bar to refill it. She sets it before him but remains standing, leaning against the bar with arms folded tight across her chest. His heart starts beating, fast, and it won't slow down. He watches bubbles rise from the bottom of his glass. "I've been happy for some time. I'm alone but I don't *need* people. It's good to see you, cousin. It is. But I don't ever need it."

She waits.

"I believe you," he says.

She nods and sits back down. "So I want you to be honest with me or I want you to leave and not come back. Tell me, Amur Ola, what's happening with you."

Once a month, for two years: she never brought it up.

She knows his surname. It pisses him off, hearing it in her mouth. Maybe she's written a relative, maybe even his mothers. He takes a sip of his beer and thinks about hurting her. Not about really doing it. About how he can.

"No, Dansia. I don't want to—"

"Don't care what you *want to*." She points to the door, squinting over her cigarette like she's aiming a crossbow. "I'm fucking serious, dead serious—you tell me or you leave. I mean, screw this *talking about it* like there's any debate. Enough, enough, *enough*. When you came here, you looked one way; there was grey in all that ridiculous white hair, wrinkles on your face. Now you look this way, like some statue of Adrash or some shit. People here don't fucking pay attention, but of course I do. Of course I do!"

"You do," he says, and he fully gets it all at once, how much of an asshole he is. Like the woman's *blind*. "I'm sorry, cousin."

He reaches into his shorts pocket and pulls out a waxpaper packet of dust. He pauses. She watches, expressionless, as he pours half of it—a sixteenth gram—into his beer, which fizzes with a radiance visible in the low light of the shuttered barroom. She wrinkles her nose at the smell, like heated metal. He drinks it slowly but without pause, looking at her through the warped bottom of the glass. He's used to the taste now, but it probably ruins the beer. Of course it does.

She shakes her head and leans forward, staring into his eyes. "How'd you *possibly* get so much , and how are you— You're mad. Cousin, I... what do you even say to this?" She sits back. Remembering her beer, she downs a quarter of it. For a moment she looks afraid. It doesn't last long. "Isn't your brain supposed to be mush by now?"

Amur shrugs. The dust is quiet. "I've been lucky, maybe. Who the fuck knows anyway; it's not like any of us really know. I feel sharper every day." His eyes rove around before landing on a portrait on the wall next to the front door. A Nosi woman, pretty in a bland way. She holds a placard beneath her chest. On it, the word *Home*. He shifts in his chair, gets up, paces around the place, and sits down again.

She reaches across the table and picks up his glass. She sniffs it, grimacing. She runs her finger around the inside of the glass, picking up grains of dust.

"I wouldn't," he says just before she pops her finger in her mouth.

She lifts her eyebrows. "You're brave, cousin, but no less a fool. Why do this? You were beautiful before, man! If not for the eyebrows, there'd be nothing left to remind me of who you were. It saddens me."

She watches him. "What, you think you can fight *him*?"

He suppresses the quick anger. That she knows his story makes him feel like a child. The question makes him feel like a child.

"Yes," he admits to her, suddenly and completely defeated. He can't duck everything. "I'm not kidding myself—I don't think. And if I do, what does it matter? I just want a chance, if only to surprise and *hurt*. I want to see that look on his face. This way is better than the other way, where I'm only a man." He lifts his chin. "I think about what I'll do before I die."

She rolls her eyes. Nosi boys talking about death is nothing new. Her gesture reminds him of someone, but he doesn't even try to summon who. It's a good association; it's not always so bad when someone treats you like a pipsqueak. Women have always humbled him.

"You want the end so badly?" she says.

He shrugs because there's no answer for it. He thinks about Sroma, alone in the cabin. He thinks about Dorone, and how Orrus might have been wrong, and how if he was wrong then there's no place far enough for them to go, he won't be able to protect her. Not for long. He thinks about her death, and he hates it. He feels obligated, like he needs to anticipate it, like he needs to keep coming back to it. He needs to be ready.

"Why would he come here, to this place. For you?" she says. "It's been *decades*, Amur."

"I have something he wants."

"The dust?"

"No."

She pours what's left of her beer in his glass, swirls it around with the grains of dust, and drinks. "I knew a woman once, he'd been contracted to an elderim. Not an important one, really, but still. He used some of the money to start a business. It helped his family. He gave the rest away."

She looks him in the eye. "That boy was young and foolish, but he wasn't a fool, not permanently."

He nods slowly, like he's really listening to her.

Grimacing, she pinches the bridge of her nose. "This is all too much, cousin. I'm going to close up for the day. You'll have to wait for your order till tomorrow morning."

"Okay. Be with you."

"With you."

Sleep eludes him. He shifts on the unfamiliar bed. He flips the pillow, mashing it into another neck-aching position. He turns on the radio. Four stations, all horrible; he listens to one idiot talk a while about football and cooking pigs underground and loving women. The air is still and it's got no salt in it. He should have gone home, come back tomorrow for the beer—he could have been home by now. He misses his armchair, his records. For one stupid second, he worries about something happening to his music journals and art folios. He imagines a fire.

He misses her, and because he's a fool he imagines her

loneliness until there's an ache in his chest, a lump in his throat. Maybe she loves when he's away. But he doesn't think so. She suffers his absence like he suffers hers. They have a life, and it could have been a different life; he doesn't have to do this thing, this mad whatever thing he's doing. He imagines Dorone stepping onto the beach. His beach. *Their beach.*

The dust refuses him tonight; no release from exhaustion, from clarity.

"Take care of her," he says. He remembers the moment, who said it. Orrus means something to her.

"It's the salt on my hands," he says because it's something he says, a song lyric maybe—he wore whatever it is down, of course he did, until all that's left is the pattern of sounds. He imagines looking at his own hand after a long day playing in the sea. The salt has dried upon it. His hand is covered in a thin layer of white dust.

"It's the salt on my hands," he says again.

He stares at the ceiling, wondering how long he can make this life last. He imagines a day when he only knows her. She takes him for a walk, and he knows only beauty and joy, endless curiosity. It lasts forever. Of course it doesn't. He thinks of her, alone. He thinks about Dorone and how, because of Dorone, he must always be waiting, living in this tension. It isn't a new thought. None of them are.

Kua, Semet al-E, Southern Ob, Iswee
(Fall—22 years old)

He looks at Orrus, looks away, looks back. The elderim is staring at the door. His features have set, impenetrable. For this, Amur is grateful. They sit together at the table, motionless. Any moment, there will be a whine, a howl—barking, growling. Now. *Now.* Instead, there's silence and the weight of silence. Amur closes his eyes, breathes deep into his belly. He tries not to think, not even one thought. He succeeds in that there are too many thoughts to isolate any *one*; his mind is deafened by feedback.

"So you like guys who hurt animals."

Amue flinches. Orrus is still staring at the door. His expression hasn't changed.

"I—"

"He's killing her, boy. And she isn't an animal."

Amur stares at the elderim. "He said she won't feel an—"

Orrus grunts. "Dead is dead. He has the words and somehow that makes it right in your mind? You're heartless, is what you are. No, you're stupid. You won't live long enough *not* to be stupid." He thumps his chest, and it sounds like a drumbeat. "What she did, those stories you tell each other about *The Hound,* she did because of *me*, because we were at *war*, because it brought me joy and so it brought her joy.

I never needed *words* to make her do a fucking *thing*. She's submitting because she has to. Otherwise—." A growl peels the lips back from his teeth so that he looks catlike, predatory. "You don't even know what she is, do you? You don't know what *anything* is here."

"I—"

"Nevermind." He looks at Amur a moment, looks back at the door. He appears briefly wistful, eyes wide, as though a memory has caught him unaware. His frown returns. "Listen, boy—"

"Don't call me boy."

Orrus cocks his head to the side, as if he's heard a voice from somewhere else. "You like this house? You think it's quaint. It was mine. I took him here, where I'd built something real for no reason other than to build it. I felt so *keen* for doing this thing no one does, at least not elderim of my stature. I filled it with things I love. This place is part of *me*, Amur. When I finally showed him it, he took it from me. One day, he was being lovely to me; the next he took from me a part of myself, you understand? And what was the slight? I took too much for *myself*. He didn't like what I'd done, for myself. And so, I handed over the keys. He can do that, you see, because of this one little quirk of fate—I'm *this* close to being him, having his power, but I was born to another father." The cables of his neck pull taut; his pulses are rabbit-fast at the base of his throat. "Anyway. That's your guy."

"I don't think that," Amur says. He blinks, his first thought having fled. "It's not quaint. I think it's beautiful." He looks away, and finds the painting. The mother and child picnicking together. "Your home, I mean. Dorone's ho…"

Orrus turns, follows his gaze. "Laj in Hora, '54, though not the '54 you're thinking of, not by a long shot. Her wife and daughter. Yes, it's true—we once had women. Maybe you knew that. They gave birth like yours do." He regards Amur.

His fingers tap on the table, a nervous rhythm. He's sharp, alert; he looks like he wants to run. Amur hopes he will.

"I need you to do something for me."

Amur looks at the door, wondering at the silence beyond it. "I'm not helping you. I'm sorry for what he's going to do."

Orrus lays his hands flat on the table. "He's already done that. She is gone, and my heart is broken. Right now, he's locating where her soul resides within her and determining how to remove it. It's a painstaking process, trickier if you're lazy like him. But he'll find it, in just a bit. He'll find the decoy we placed in her spine. We worked hard on it, it passses close scrutiny, and he's a fool anyway—all he wants is to possess her, him and no one else. Simply because he can, and I love her, and he's *bored*. He doesn't even *know* her. He'll—"

Dorone's voice, but faint. Chanting? Louder now.

Cursing.

Orrus grins. "He'll be fooled because I'm *not* a fool and he doesn't understand a fucking thing about her."

He pauses, listening perhaps. He breathes deeply, shakes his head.

"This is what's going to happen: I'm going to remove her soul from her body. I'm going to place it under her. You're going to retrieve it. When you're ready, but not when you're an old man, you're going to revive her."

Amur opens his mouth, closes it. What Orrus said is preposterous. "She's dangerous. She's... it's a *weapon*. It *should* be in Dorone's care."

Orrus huffs. "Spare me, boy. *Amur*. You don't understand what's happening, not at all. That's not your fault. Yes, she is dangerous. Don't give her dust but once when you revive her, but use a fair bit then. It's potent, not anything like your Noerre stuff. Go somewhere far away and just live. Let her live. You'll need a body, just put her soul in its mouth. Don't look at me that way, like it's crazy. You live in the world, you see who we are, what we can do. Yes, I know your people. I know what you think of us." He smiles with that trace of wistfulness. "You're not far wrong. Oftentimes. But we aren't *so unalike*. I know this. I just don't care. But you, somehow. She—" His mouth works at it before he can say it. "She likes you. And so I changed my plan. *We* changed it."

"What?"

"She's chosen you."

"Chosen?" The dog—the *Hound*. An Elder relic. Amur refuses to think about it. "No."

"Yes."

"*No*," he says.

It happens between blinks: Orrus reaches across the table and grips Amur's wrists. Amur pulls back, but there's no budging. Nonetheless, the grip is gentle. Amur meets the elderim's gaze. Orrus nods as if they've come to an agreement.

"Life is not some story right now, Amur. It's not a long-ago war between our people. This—all of this, you and Dorone—it's nothing to him. I'm offering you something more, something new. You're going to do it, Amur. I know because she chose you. Take care of her."

Amur shakes his head. He stares at Orrus's hands around his wrists. He stares at the ridiculous pink bracelet and feels like a child. He is a child. All men are children here, in this place. He thinks of home. He sees Marus sitting next to his dog. He wants to go home, even where it hurts. It'll be hard enough on his own.

"I can't."

The grip tightens incrementally until the bones of Amur's wrists bend and creak, until he gasps. Orrus shakes his head. "Think about it, man. He's taken you with him, here, to do this awful useless thing because he *can*. He's hurting me in front of you, his lover. He's told you a story about how this *matters*, about how the fucking symbolism of it. It's all *symbols*. If he were serious he'd do more than offer up a body without a soul, without *her*. It amuses him to pretend with you, with them, with all your people. How long have you known him, *man*? You're in my home, a home I built before you were even a *thought* of a *thought*. Listen to me. Think about what it means that he took you here, to some place that means nothing to him and everything to me—and that he lied to you so casually about it!" He looks to the door again. He listens. "That's all the advice you'll get, I'm afraid. I don't have time."

A loud crack from outside, like wood splitting. Amur flinches. Orrus loosens his grip and stands. When he speaks, his voice is flat. "There's a ten-kilo brick of bonedust in the hidden drawer of my desk. Under the left set of drawers. The dust is shielded, inert, and strongly warded; do not attempt to open it by force or you will die. The words to open it are inscribed on the box, simple Elder words. It's more than any man has ever owned or will own. Take it, rule a country somewhere. Take care of her. She likes the ocean."

Amur stares at Orrus's tightly clenched fists. He looks at the door. He thinks about it. He thinks about a *dog*.

Orrus snaps his fingers. "Like *that*, and I can make you gone. Fucking say it."

Amur nods. "Yes." He may mean it.

Orrus waits until Amur meets his gaze, and holds it a moment before nodding. "Keep her away from elderim. Keep her away from it all. Let her run, be a man's creature." He walks to the door. His armor flows like liquid over his body, sheathing him in matte gold until only his upper chest, shoulders, neck, and head are free of it.

"Wait," Amur says as the elderim is opening the front door.

He has questions, suddenly, as if they've been waiting for this moment. He's clear headed and very afraid.

Orrus turns. He is beautiful, resplendent in the sunlight through the screen door, and Amur is briefly struck dumb.

"Just speak, boy—Amur."

"How do you know I'll do it?"

"I don't. But you're going to want it. Something of your own, after this is over."

"He'll find it. If I take it."

"No, he won't. Not it. Her. *When* you take it."

Orrus kneels next to the Hound's body. His lips move in a regular cadence—a recitation, perhaps a prayer. Dorone watches, forearms crossed, mouth set in a hard line. Amur stands, fixed in place a few steps from the porch, gaze shifting between the two.

Orrus leans forward, cups the Hound's head, and presses his forehead to hers. He takes her massive body into his golden arms, rises, and walks further up the beach. The Hound's feet drag in the sand. Orrus continues until he's reached an outcropping of grey stone. He deposits her behind it.

Amur flinches when Dorone clears his throat.

"The point of that, Orrus?"

Orrus turns to him. His pretty face is twisted; his lips peel back from his teeth, canines flashing. "Don't want you even *looking* at her," he says. The air over his head and shoulders wavers. "I would've forgiven anything. Anything else. Really, Dorone. I *have* forgiven so many things."

Dorone uncrosses his arms. "She's gone. *Don't*, Orrus."

Orrus stares at Dorone. He slowly lifts his hands—naked, Amur sees now—from the hound's body. The armor covers his hands again.

Amur watches, caught between realizations too awful to bear.

(They're in the backyard together, Marus's uncle's backyard. They haven't kissed yet. It's about to happen. The dog is panting between them, grinning because it's alive and loved. "Why does he lick your hands so much?" he asks. Marus grins at the dog. "It's the salt on my hands.")

(The sting of Okin's slap. "Enough of this, boy, all this fantasy shit!" She tears his drawings off the walls, his meticulous sketches of black and brown and cream and purple skinned men in glorious armor fighting, kissing, living their lives. She crumples them in her fists. Broken inside, he stares at her, that familiar pressure in his throat, that wetness in the corners of his eyes. He's too silly; he's always showing how he knows nothing. "Pay attention!" his mother shouts. "Fucking things are happening in the world!")

Orrus steps toward Dorone. Under his naked feet, the sand catches fire and turns to glass, pinging like stressed metal. Wisps of white smoke curl from his fists. Measured steps, gaze locked on Dorone. His irises have disappeared, leaving his eyes the color of snow, of iron heated to the point it begins to crumble.

"Orrus," Dorone says. "No."

Orrus smiles, nods *yes yes*, and slaps his chest. Even from quite far away, the heat of his rage forces Amur back toward the porch. He lifts his foot, misses the step, and lands on his back. By the time he's raised his head, Orrus is in motion—an indistinct golden shape arrowing toward Dorone. Amur flinches, expecting the crack of dust-strengthened bodies colliding. But Dorone evades the blow, the only sign of his maneuver the dust rising from his feet. Orrus reengages, landing a glancing blow to Dorone's shoulder before taking Dorone's elbow to the left cheek. Orrus's head snaps back and he retreats, circling clockwise.

Eyes fixed on Dorone's face, Orrus curls his shoulders like boxers do. Dorone appears calm but alert—*keen* even, like a cat watching crippled prey. He turns in place, balance weighted on his back foot. He keeps his eyes on Orrus's body.

Orrus darts forward and commits. Amur stands and steps forward, into the blistering heat, overawed despite his fear.

The superficial appearance of men, the suggestion of similar lineage, vanishes from the elderim. Men can't move this way. Men are too fragile; just moving this fast will shatter their bones. He tries to follow the blurred, arcing movements of the elderims' arms, the sweeping motions of their kicks, the sudden thrusts of their knees. They dance, darting in and out of reach, rarely able to land more than a glancing blow on the other. Orrus is knocked to the ground twice, once hurled into a small tree that cracks and falls under his weight. His face is a fierce mask, teeth bared like an animal. The muscles stand out on his frame, twitching and swollen under the sheen of his armor. He disengages briefly and circles Dorone, feet in constant motion, turning his calves white with sand. Then back in. Longer armed but equally as quick as Dorone, every punch looks as though it will land. Those that do land are devastating, their sound like rocks splitting. Dorone has been knocked back twice, though not to the ground. He's always just out of reach or fractionally bent away from Orrus's fists. He betrays no emotion, shifting from foot to foot but keeping his weight on the back foot. An Isweean style, unlike anything Amur has seen. He deflects most blows easily, as if he's simply slapping Orrus's hands to the side. His offense consists principally of kicks; he times them precisely, shifting weight suddenly when Orrus comes in close and aiming for the knee.

There!

Orrus shouts and falls back, limping on his left leg.

Belatedly, Amur hears the snap. There's a dent in Orrus's shin: a fracture or break. No man could stand on it.

The armor smooths over the dent, sets the bone. Orrus howls.

"That's it," Dorone says. *"Mercy.* Ask for it, maybe you'll live. Diminished, but alive."

Orrus smiles and stamps the heel of his crippled leg into the ground. He howls again, like a dog in pain. White smoke lifts from his hands, his bowed shoulders. The armor masks his head and his eyes burn white hot.

Dorone shakes his head. "Waste."

Amur barely registers the transition. Between one blink and the next, the blue scales of Dorone's armor multiply, spreading over his torso and legs, arms and head, enveloping him in its skin-tight embrace. His eyes flare, once, twice, a third time dazzlingly. Amur blinks away the light blindness.

Orrus stands tall, on unshaking legs. *:You need that so early, do you.:* Contempt warps his features under the armor. *:There was a time when you could beat me without it. You're getting old, Dorone—the dust is ready to move on.:*

:I don't wish to belabor this, Orrus. I've no desire to add to your pain.:

Amur grits his teeth; a pathetic sound slips past his lips. Both elderim are speaking the not-speak, with words that hammer against the walls of Amur's skull. Such speech is common enough among the elderim that Amur has become used to it; hearing a skilled elderim singer with your ears while your mind hears that same voice countersinging is shiver inducing. Dorone uses the voice with Amur rarely, softly, and only in moments of intimacy. But this—*this* is violence.

Orrus laughs. A tired sound, like he's heard a tired joke. His armor amplifies it; the laughter booms in the air, an awful sound. "Pain. One has to experience it to know what it means.

You've grown *nothing* of your own, ever. You've never done anything that *could* hurt." He tilts his head back and stares at the sky. He spreads his arms wide and leans backwards. Light leaks from between his clenched fingers. White smoke pours from his eyes. The heat redoubles. Amur's ears pop.

"The dust moves on, Dorone." Orrus lowers his head. "I move on. You move—"

Dorone throws up his arms.

A star rips through Orrus. The world disappears in white fire.

At fourteen he took his first real job, as a courier, biking the morning route into neighboring Kredwan and Shorm, twin cities twenty kilometers northeast of Jalast, across the mesa, near the salt plains. They weren't big cities, but they were new, comparatively, immigrant places—Kredwan founded by Ulome, Shorm by northern Tomen. The streets confused him, and he was too proud to ask directions.

He'd gotten turned around in Shorm, and there was a street market he'd passed, but it didn't seem like the right one ("Head east on Avri, second left after the *fruit* market"), and now he couldn't find it again.

Madness; had he pedaled clear out of his own country? Why would anyone make their streets and homes so straight, so bare and similar? Didn't these people know about trees, different color paint and brick? He didn't like peering up so much, having these buildings loom over him. If he really looked he saw the ornamentation; he saw how precise and *clean* everything was, how friendly everyone was.

But still; it was like being surrounded by hills or trees all the time, closed in. The vast blooming plains of the mesa, the snow-capped mountain ranges he'd known his whole life—

these people put buildings in the way! You couldn't build above two stories in Jalast. Unless you were a school or a church.

He looked down at the letter in his hand, now smudged and warped. He wiped his palms on his shorts and slapped a mosquito on his forearm. He reached beneath his waistband and scratched his balls, adjusting himself. He was dressed only in black shorts, tight and spare like he liked them. He looked naked, and people stared. His temples were shaved and the rest grew longer than his middle finger. He was always running his hands through it, pulling out strands of big white curls, stretching them out and letting them bounce back to his head. His sisters told him he was the vainest person ever, and he couldn't argue.

His hair was disgusting now. It was dusty and hot and humid. The sun hung directly overhead and rational folks were inside or at least under shade.

"You lost?"

Amur looked up. He'd stopped, wasn't paying attention. *Vedas*, it was hot under the sun. A shirtless boy, lighter skinned and freckled, sat on the stoop of a three-storey tenement across the street. A small black and brown dog sat at his side.

"Nah," Amur said. "I'm just around the corner. I think. I can find it."

The boy laughed and stepped into the road. Amur watched him and his dog cross the pavement. The dog reached Amur first and circled, barking. The boy told it to shut up, but he laughed when he said it and the dog listened. He wore short, loose pants that came to mid calf and nothing else—not even sandals. Tightly curled blonde hair, skin the color of wet sand. Freckles everywhere but especially across the bridge of his nose. Pale green eyes.

"Don't worry. I can find it," Amur said. He put his foot on the pedal.

"No problem. Where you going?" He was shorter than Amur by a few centimeters. Still, Amur guessed he was a year or two older.

Amur showed him the letter.

The boy smiled. There was a slight gap between his two front teeth. Amur's heart throbbed in the hollow of his throat. He stared at the boy's tightly muscled chest, his small reddish nipples and his lean belly. He stared at the boy's dirty feet. His face grew warm and he looked away. He was still unused to the signs, but he guessed the boy was from the south, as far as Rash-Toma maybe. Not a face you saw in Jalast.

He'd never paid attention to why Okin hated Tomen so much. Not in particular. She had the same reasons as everyone.

"You're almost where you gotta be," this boy said. "I like your face. I like your hair. What's your name?"

Amur met the boy's gaze, looked away again. This boy *stared*. Nosi boys didn't look at one another like that, not right off, not without some sort of joke, some sign it's cool to be taking in *so much* of you. Amur wasn't ready for any of it, even though he'd seen it all his life; blame his sisters, who talked of nothing but sex and made him feel like a freak for being so tall, so beautiful, so obsessed with his own body. They made fun of him because he was afraid, because he was a big talker about everything but sex.

Big tough boy Amur. So fast, so strong. Such a wimp.

"Thank you," Amur said. He pressed his palm to his chest. "Amur. You... What's your name?"

The boy stepped forward, closer than Amur was used to among strangers. Amur didn't step back, however. He caught the scent of some fragrant food, spices he couldn't name, and the sharp tang of dried sweat. He felt the first tinglings and clamped down, hard. He was *digging* this boy. And he didn't dig boys. He turned *down* boys. Men, on the other hand... he'd almost gotten himself in trouble, a few times.

"Marus," the boy said. "From my uncle."

Amur barely listened to Marus's directions and looked like a fool when he couldn't repeat them back. In the end, the boy walked Amur there. The destination was less than five minutes away. The boy talked to him. Amur answered. Maybe he did. He waited in the chemist's while the order was prepared, annoyed it was taking so long but also relieved. The boy stood around for a minute or two and then walked away. Amur thought about how, next time, he'd tell the boy his name.

"Marus," Amur said on the way back to Jalast. "Marus. Marus, Marus. Hey, Marus. I'm Amur. I'm Amur. I am *Amur*."

He returned to Shorm the following week with another order for the chemist. The streets confounded him again, but he remembered Marus's street. He was disappointed to find the stoop empty. Disappointed and relieved. He never even got that close to the building; the idea of Marus seeing him from inside horrified him, for some reason.

He returned again two days later; he made the twenty-kilometer trip on his one day off, with nothing to deliver. He ate at a noodle place and ordered a second serving. Working up his nerve.

The dog found him first. The boy grinned and Amur's heart fluttered.

They were in the backyard, a small space enclosed by cement walls. The fruit market was just over the other side of the north wall, but the cement was thick, shielding them from most of the noise. It was muggy, but they sat close together, nearly hidden from sight in the dense garden Maru's uncles kept.

Marus's family—three uncles, one papa, Marus's two brothers, and two other lighter skinned folks whose names Amur couldn't pronounce—had welcomed Amur into their home with no ceremony. Mother Chora would've been scandalized: no getting to know this new boy, just, *Sure, what's one more around here*? It was loud in the two-bedroom flat, filled with man sounds. It stunk like Amur's room.

Did they care that he was Nosi? No way to tell. They commented on his hair but not on his skin or accent, and Amur wondered if the whole world worked more like this than he'd imagined. To hear his mothers tell it, the world was made of walls.

He was quiet around them, no kind of loudmouth, and charming as could be. He grew embarrassed when he thought of Agra seeing him, being so demure. Once, he overheard a conversation that stopped when he entered the main room to use the bathroom. He heard them say Noerre, and weean. He wasn't a fool. Okin talked politics all the time. Everyone else listened.

Amur rubbed the dog's belly and found he liked it. His mothers had never allowed pets, and the idea that anyone, anywhere, would allow an animal other than an itinerant tabby into their home, moreover treat it as a companion, shocked him. Of course he'd met other people with dogs; it wasn't an *impossible* thing, merely odd. Agra loved dogs; she squealed like a kid when she saw one, and she never squealed.

But he'd never met *this* boy. He'd never seen someone so fixated on an animal, like it was a person. Marus plotted revenge on folks who kept their dogs chained up all day. His boldness made Amur feel stuttery and coltish. He didn't always hate it.

"Why do you look at him so much?" he asked.

"Dunno. Seems obvious," Marus said. He furrowed his brow in a way Amur liked; he had more lines on his face than most boys, but he was two weeks younger than Amur. He stared at the dog, lips quirked in amusement. The dog looked at him, panting. It trusted Marus; he was its leader, hanging on every word he spoke.

"Reft's not like us. His thoughts are *wild*. Why wouldn't I look at him so much?"

"And he just follows you? He doesn't run away? Why's he licking your hands so much?"

Marus grinned at the dog. "It's the salt on my hands. I heard that once, and he definitely likes salt. And he loves me. He can't get enough of me." He met Amur's gaze and winked. "That happens sometimes with me."

Amur laughed when he understood it was a joke. "You mean—"

The boy was reaching to touch Amur's hair, and Amur only just kept himself from slapping the hand away. His whole life, people were touching his hair.

"Is this okay?" Marus asked.

Amur nodded and closed his eyes as Marus's fingers moved in his hair. He lowered his head until his chin rested on his chest. His head bobbed to the delirious beating of his heart, and for a moment his body wanted to *move*, to be anywhere but here.

Marus scooted closer until their hips were pressed together. He turned toward Amur and used both hands to massage his scalp.

The sight of the boy's bare chest and freckled shoulders, the muscle moving underneath his smooth skin. The lower half of his smiling face, the gap between his two front teeth. The smell of him, like dirt and dried sweat and food and dog.

"Lift your head," Marus said.

"What?" Amur said. He was afraid to lift his head, the boy was so close.

"Why?" he asked.

"So I can kiss you," the boy said.

•

Nosi mothers aren't known for their indulgence, especially to their sons, but Amur was past the age his mothers insisted he keep curfew. Point in fact, they and his sisters liked him out of the house—him and his man stink. He'd tested out of summer classwork the prior year, leaving him with the kind of freedom only wealthy daughters had.

He still had to be careful. He was savvy in a certain way, more private than his peers, because he'd always been recognized everywhere he went. He had a loud mouth and a temper. Each time he visited Marus, he wore a headwrap like he'd turned devout and took a different route out of town. Paranoia; maybe not. Marus kept track of the extra kilometers Amur traveled to get to him; he wrote them on the cement wall behind where they first kissed.

They didn't talk about why it must be this way because neither of them was stupid. Marus knew Amur was the only boy in his house, that his family was Northern with a capital N and filled with women. He didn't know Amur's mothers' names, his sisters' names. It didn't matter; Marus would never know them. Marus had never set foot in Jalast, and his family rarely traveled to Danoor except on holidays.

He talked a lot about Noerre, or at least his idea of the mines.

"You all used to make *bombs* there," he said. There was a game called bombs; every kid knew it, as basic as games get. Amur had a sister named Noerre. Marus talked about the war like he never once thought to ask if his teachers were full of shit. When Amur thought of war, he thought of being hurt so badly he couldn't move. War was good for no one. War was a *past* subject, for books.

"You really would blow it all up before surrendering it, wouldn't you?" Marus said.

Amur nodded. Of that, he was sure. He didn't like the look on Marus's face when they talked about it. Marus made fun of northerners—the same jokes everyone told, all the old assumptions: Nosi are arrogant, they have shitty senses of humor, they're food is so spicy you can't eat it. (These are not entirely untrue statements.) But he also glorified them. His idea of northerners, of Nosi in general. The only nation that had kept some of its power, the only people who'd stood up to *them*.

It was annoying. He was so damn hot, though. In all other ways, he was utterly radiant.

"I heard all that shit before," Amur told him. "So let's not talk about it. C'mere..."

Marus called himself a punk, a word Amur knew and sort of understood. It meant something different in Jalast, where only girls called themselves punks and didn't seem interested in sharing whatever they'd found. He'd always dug their rooster-dos, though, and their ripped up pants.

For Marus, punk meant everything. His uncle Oran had a record player and Marus had only one record, a band called Sauna Youth; Amur hated it viscerally but loved how much joy it brought Marus, who wanted punk to be everything to Amur.

"You need to come with me tonight—same guys I played, Sauna Youth. So good. They *live* here, you know, all that way. We're lucky."

Amur was skeptical. The music was terrible. And he didn't want to be seen in public too much, especially not in big crowds. Marus said it was unlikely anyone from Jalast would be there, which was true. Of course.

"Not cool enough," Marus said, and grinned. "Except *you*, obviously."

The venue was dark, cavernous, and echoing, filled near to bursting with teens. Most were around Amur's age; no one looked over the age of twenty. He got a lot of stares but didn't see any Nosi. The band members—a guitarist, a bassist, a drummer, all guys, and a small, severe-looking woman with a microphone and keyboard—were older, maybe in their twenties, and looked nothing like the local kids; they were easterners, pale-skinned and dressed in plaid shirts and sweaters and knit pants. Uptight people clothes.

Once they got going, though, they transformed. The guitarist and the keyboardist shouted their words together, like they were pissed off at everything. They abused their patched and mended instruments, pulling out razor-sharp sounds unlike anything Amur had ever heard. The crowd shouted back with equal force and abandon. They were like animals. They looked ridiculous and embarrassing.

It was just ugliness and violence, that first time. Whenever Marus wasn't looking, Amur clapped his hands over his ears. He felt the kick drum in his guts, like being punched over and over again, and for a moment he thought he was going to throw up.

Why would *anyone* make such noise? The racket left no room to breathe, barely enough space to think. He was relieved when the set ended and they left the overcrowded club full of sweaty, shirtless kids. They flowed into the night, mohawked and spiky-haired, shouting and air guitaring under the streetlights. Amur's head rang and he was a little stoned; the smoke was thick in there, funky as hell.

Marus drew him into an alley; they kissed and used their hands and came on each others' bellies, and Marus whispered, his breath smelling like Amur, "Wasn't that *amazing*?"

Bullshit, Amur thought, but soon it was: by the third show, the noise started to make sense. He felt it in his bones, the need to move. By the fifth show, he wanted to hear nothing else. He abandoned his body to the galloping beat, losing himself in two-minute bursts of wiry tension. It was during his eighth show that he lost himself. (A band called Broken Water, unbearably cacophonous, like a mountain falling on you; the drummer got so hot that she stripped and played in her chonies.) He ripped his head wrap off and threw it over the raised fists. Marus shouted something. Amur missed it, but it hardly mattered. Marus's face shined. They danced and threw punches in the air. When the song was over they hugged and kissed and groped each other, disgusting as hell, covered in their sweat, other kids' sweat. Amur bled from a cut on his temple and now had a streak of red running through his hair. A few boys told him they liked what he'd done to it. They thought he'd bleached it, and told him it looked cool, and for a moment he knew what it was like to be young and beautiful and *that's it*; he wasn't a cousin or a nephew or a son, recognizable by everyone everywhere he went. He wasn't expected to be anything.

On the way back to Marus's place, Amur drew Marus into a church's entryway. He knelt and gave Marus a messy blowjob, aware of how visible they were, how someone could pass by even at that hour. He chose not to care. He rose and they kissed, tasting like cum.

"I love you," Marus said.

"I love you too," Amur said, breathless.

He returned two days later, as soon as his courier schedule and chores allowed. They ate with Marus's family. After dinner, they took Reft for a walk alongside the central canal, one of the few open spaces in town. The walkways on either bank were busy with people, but they barely noticed. The sun was descending and a cool breeze came through. The dog was delirious with joy, a total awkward fool, sniffing everything, pissing on the purple-blooming germanders. Amur and Marus held hands. It was three days short of four months since they met. Marus had kept track.

On the way back, Amur directed Marus into a long dirt alleyway behind some restaurants. It was a Tuesday and a fast day, so the restaurants were closed. Amur kissed the boy he loved. He had a song stuck in his head, just the one winding melody over and over again—*I try to leave, I try to leave, I try to leave...*

The dog barked.

Five girls stepped into the alley.

Amur recognized them. Shaved temples. Punks, but not from here. From Jalast. They were all younger and smaller than Amur, but that was inconsequential. They were sharp, though a couple of them looked pretty scared. They'd come with cricket bats and chains, and the angle of the alley prevented anyone from seeing inside. It was a fast day, not a lot of people around this area. Amur thought of shouting, and how he probably should. If he were in Jalast... This wouldn't be happening in Jalast.

"Heya, stonecutter," one of the girls said. She smiled a pretty smile. She was taller than the others. Her name was on the tip of Amur's tongue. Agra knew her. A rival.

"You gotta go," he told Marus. He looked behind them. There was an exit.

He didn't think. He raised his voice. It wasn't a performance.

"This is over." He stared at the girls rather than Marus; he looked at the girls' fists. "I'm serious, Marus. We're done. Go away."

"What?" Marus said.

"Yeah, *what?*" one of the girls shouted. They laughed. They didn't sound like they were going to wait long.

"Get fucking *lost*," Amur said to Marus. "Go. The Fuck. Away."

But Marus stood, confused, the dog pulling him toward the girls. Amur looked Marus in the eye, saw the hurt on his face, but by then Amur was already in motion, running straight for the girls. One of them had moved, he was sure.

"Go!" he shouted. "*Go, fucking go!*"

But Reft lunged, tearing the lead from Marus's hands, and reached the girls before Amur. The tall girl swung her bat and hit the dog in the ribs, sending it tumbling across the ground. Reft hit the restaurant wall and lay still. Marus screamed as Amur leapt, arms spread wide, carrying the tall girl to the ground. He took an elbow to the cheek but rolled to the side and rose. He placed himself between Marus and the girls.

"Go," he told Marus.

"No! Reft—"

"Go!"

Marus sprinted and picked up his dog. It made no sound.

"I'm sorry," Amur said, but the words were lost and no use anyway. The boy was gone.

One of the girls jumped to give chase, but Amur tackled her. He grabbed her hair and slammed her head into the dirt. The tall girl landed on his back and he hurled her off. She came back quicker than he imagined. She was fast, Agra fast. He knocked her down twice and she just snarled and got back up.

For a moment he had the upper hand. Then the other three found their eggs and crowded in, swinging their bats and chains.

Of course someone told his mothers, or his sisters. Maybe Okin had sent the girls; it was the sort of thing she and Mambee would do. He was scared to death of Grandma Mambee; scared more of her than Okin. They'd once had a girl beaten for spreading a rumor about Jen losing her virginity to a southern boy. The southern boy—who knows what happened to the southern boy. No son or grandson of theirs would be seen with a Tomen. There would be an accounting. He knew this, like he knew the sun would rise.

He waited a full hour after his mothers' bedtime, climbed the wall to the backyard, and snuck to his room. He didn't sleep, not really. He limped into the kitchen the next morning. He wore a skirt, no shirt. He refused to lower his head or look ashamed. It wasn't easy. He was covered in purple bruises, but at least he'd kept most of the blows from his face.

"Come here," Chora said from the dining table. She examined his face. She put her fingers in his hair to feel the lumps. She pressed each wound on his arms and torso, making him turn in place to examine them all. She took his face between her hands and slapped him, lightly, on either cheek.

"Cocky little shit," she said. "Foolish boy."

"Traitor," Okin announced. Her heavy hand fell on his shoulder. She squeezed until he cried out. "Got better than you deserve."

Chora clucked her tongue. "Foolish," she repeated. "Love boys—we don't care. Of course we don't. But come home after dirtying your prick again with..." She turned to the side, sticking her tongue out as though vomiting.

Okin moved faster than the eye could follow, striking Chora in the sternum. Chora fell off her chair and lay gasping on the floor. Okin stood, placing her hands on the table, leaning over Amur. He didn't move, didn't breathe.

"Your mother makes a joke of this," Okin said. "I do not. What are you?"

"What?" he said.

Okin slapped him, rocking his head to the side. The room swam. "What are you?"

He paused.

She slapped him again, knocking him from his seat. "Get up. Now. What are you?"

He let the blood run from his nose. "Nosi."

Okin cupped a hand around her ear. "I'm sorry. What did you say?"

"Nosi, *sir*."

He flinched as her finger stabbed his forehead. "You make no decisions with *this*, boy. Not your eyes, not your cock." She grabbed his wrist and squeezed, grinding the bones of his wrist together. "Your fate is here, in what runs through your veins."

"Yes, Mama."

She let go. "You fuck only who your blood tells you to fuck. You love only who your blood tells you to love. I don't care if the king of Casta Setjis propositions you; it's not your choice. No exceptions, or you walk out of this house a stranger. Today you will visit Mambee and apologize. When you are done with that, you will go to your aunts' houses and apologize. People will see you do it. Tell everyone you see that you're apologizing. Tell me you fucking understand."

"Yes, Mama."

"Yes, what?"

"I understand."

Prota, Medile Sea
(Winter—47 years old—3 years old)

After two months of grey hell, the storms lift, revealing the moonless sky and the vast, starry swath of the Arc passing straight overhead. He breathes fuller and deeper. He opens his eyes wider; his nose twitches to capture the freshness of it. He takes Sroma on a walk, south along the sloped shore strewn with bladderwrack and small sharp shells. The air becomes sluggish, filled with a salty funk, like a man's underarm. It smells good. He shivers and gets hard goosebumps everywhere. His hands rove over his body like it's someone else's.

Tonight, he says to himself, *I won't take it.*

It's been four years; has he even once missed a dose? The fear of it is strong but the desire for change is stronger, so he follows it. Winters are hard; the days are short and he misses the sun on his skin. He doesn't need it; he's never cold.

He hasn't been kind lately. Not to her, not to himself.

They step close enough to Merit to see its lit windows. That's enough, just to know there are people here. He crouches next to her, watching her profile in the dark. Her eyes are alive. He loses himself in their baleful glow. He blinks out of it and stands, head thrown back to take in the Arc, struck by its vastness, its pointilated beauty. The sky is nowhere near this brilliant in the desert, he recalls; the stars are fewer and the

Arc is rarely in full view. But he aches for it, a sky that goes on and on, and his chest swells. He crouches next to her again, watches her a while.

"Okay," he eventually says. She barks and spins in place; he ducks in time to avoid getting slapped by her tail. "Let's go home." She tears off, but into the forest. He grins. It's not a long wait. He takes the branch she's found. A good, strong one. He hurls it. She catches it, every time, no matter where he throws it.

"Yah!" he shouts. *"Good* girl!"

Home, he gives her a tendon and smokes a joint, which rarely happens anymore, but he's worried about not being able to sleep without it. The weed is dry as tinder and he doesn't get much out of it, but he still smiles in that fuzzy-headed way, like he's remembering some other time he got high. He stands in the bathroom, staring at himself in the mirror, watching the way the light plays off his skin. His face, so familiar as to almost confuse him. He stares mostly at the muscles of his chest, his shoulders, the first two rows of abdominals. He flexes like he's twenty again. It's not a large mirror and suddenly he longs for a full-length one—a luxury he once permitted himself (maybe, if he were wise). He turns and leans awkwardly, looking over his shoulder to get a look at his ass. He slaps it so it jiggles, and the high hits him all at once. He sways, presses a hand to the sink to steady himself. He strokes himself hard and watches himself come.

He enters the bedroom and sits on the floor. He stares at his arrangement, so carefully maintained—the small display of statues here, in the wood-and-glass bookshelf; his favorite armchair; his second-favorite chair with the band stickers all over it; and the stack of records leaning against the wall. He selects one—Ice Baths' *Decadent Sprinter*—and shakes his butt to the familiar monochrome beat. He puts on Perfect Aesthetic's *Opposite of Lovers* and nods his head hard, fighting back tears. He straightens the sheets on the bed. The record ends and he turns on the radio, knowing it'll just be static. He listens to the static. He turns off the radio.

He starts thinking about it, the decision he's made, and nearly lets himself think about it more. His body stiffens and he suddenly feels fragile, like it's all about to come apart unless he addresses it *now*. He wrenches his mind in the other direction, a practiced move.

"Girl," he says, and she comes in, panting like she's been playing but she's only just come from the other room. Also, it's quite cold. He grins at her. "Weirdo," he says, the ridiculousness of her appearance suddenly so obvious. A beast, in a man's home! How did people ever get to the point of saying, *Let us make friends with these wolves. What can go wrong?* He giggles at the absurdity of it. She licks his face and tries to sit in his lap. He moves her around until her head is nestled in the crook of his knee. He strokes her forehead, massages the velvet tips of her ears. She blinks, staring up at him, eyes dimmed to an amber glow.

"Fuck," he says to her. "I'm stupid high, like a fucking *kid*."

He pets her. He massages down the length of her spine, taking joy in the texture of her fur between his fingers, like grass, and the feeling of his own muscles lengthening and contracting. A familiar movement, like sanding wood or polishing stone. She grins wide, panting, half her tongue on the floor.

"Hold up," he tells her. He puts on another record, Deaf Wish's *On*. It's a noisy one so he turns it way down. He knows every song so well, on every record, the cracks and pops as familiar as the music itself. He wishes for more, or that he takes better care of the ones he has. Sometimes he hears new things in the music, but most of the time it's like remembering more than hearing; at the best times he allows himself to just feel whatever he feels, no filter on it.

"Orrus," he says. Her ears perk up, but she keeps her eyes closed. He's not sure why he's said it. "Someone touched you this way before. Someone loved you. I know that. *Orrus*. Yeah, you remember. I don't. Not really. The facts of it but none of the color. *Him*, of course—it takes no pushing to do it, to think of him, to sustain him in my mind. I *am* sure of him, and that saddens me. But your guy? I could see his face, not so long ago. He asked me to, he told me to, and I couldn't love *him* anymore, so I did it. Is love even what I meant to say? I didn't ever *love* him, did I? I love *you*. But eventually I did it. What he told me to do. Something like that." He sighs, then grins. "It's like I'm forgetting things!" He digs his fingers into her ribs where she's ticklish. Her back legs kick and she growls. He chuckles and lays back on the hard floor. All of the sudden he licks his palm.

A boy sitting on a stoop. A small black and brown dog sitting next to him, grinning.

"No," he says.

He starts to cry and cries for a while, quietly, wondering at the ache in his chest—he is filled with curiosity but so frightened of scaring it away, whatever he's found. He wants to see it again, whatever it is he's seen, the boy on the stoop, the black and brown dog... but there's no way to summon it that won't destroy it. He must wait, and he may wait forever.

Sroma raises her head. Crying always bugs her. He tells her it's fine and she knows he's lying. She growls, barks once softly, and lays her head back down.

The crack of thunder wakes him. The cabin creaks like it's been struck. Sroma growls, hackles raised. A second crack. He ducks. Not thunder—louder, sharper, a clap from God's hands. Sroma turns to him, whining sharply. She barks at him twice and scrambles off her bed, tearing out of the bedroom. She barks at the front door once, twice, three times, and then she shouts, she tells him GET UP.

He doesn't think, isn't allowed it; he scrambles four-legged off the bed, sprints to the door, and opens it. She shoots out into the cold black night and he follows, slipping and landing awfully on the frost-slick porch stairs. The click of his tailbone breaking, the seering *oh fucking god* pain of it, but he's already up again and after her, toes slipping for purchase on the frozen ground, up the bluff to the north, toward the ruins of Qemet. He moves like an elderim and still wills himself faster, *fastest*, sprinting across the grassy flats, leaping chasms cut into the bluff rather than going the long way round. When the way becomes rocky, he's slowed but only minimally; he moves like he's been watching her do it, but still his mind chides, *Too slow, too slow.*

By the time he reaches Qemet, his shins and feet are bruised and bloody. He bends over, heaving—he throws up. He takes great gasping breaths until his voice works.

"Girl!" he yells. *"Sroomaaaaa!"*

He finds her standing at the northernmost point, where the seawall extends, staring at the sky, sniffing the air like she's searching.

No. She recognizes something, like when she's caught the scent of prey in the forest nearby. He stops with a distance still between them. He looks into the crumbling city like he's afraid Adrash will walk out.

"Girl?" He follows her gaze into the sky. "What the f—"

Sroma's head swivels; he follows her gaze as a star shoots out of the clouds in the east, spearing into the clear, moonlit span overhead, dragging a tail of fire. After a moment, a second star emerges, trailing fire.

"Fuck," he whispers. He imagines the elderim sealed in their sleek armor, assured of their strength. Their course shifts abruptly, though; instead of falling upon Quemet, they descend beyond the trees, beyond the mountains, toward the center of the island. Amur imagines them landing like hammers upon the city, standing in the midst of wreckage, standing on what used to be Dansia's place. Their armor retreats from their faces. The elderim close their eyes, sniffing the air avidly.

The wind shifts and Sroma's heat hits him full force, like he's sitting at a campfire. There's a new smell to her, like burnt hair and struck flint.

(They're walking along the beach, he and the two elderim. The Hound comes up to him, tongue wagging.)

"Girl." His own voice surprises him. "No."

She ignores him. Nose to the sky. The sound of her sniffing. The low rumble of a growl.

"Girl..."

She howls.

He falls to his knees, filled with the noise of it, like no noise she's ever made or a man has ever heard, not language, not music, not any animal sound. He claps his hands to his ears but the noise doesn't stop, doesn't even diminish. He hunches over, knees in his belly, rocking forward and back, tears spilling onto his naked thighs. Tears, like there's no way they can ever be stopped, like his body will run out. "Orrus," he says. "Orrus, Orrus, Orrus, Orrus." He pictures the elderim like he's looking at him, like no time has passed. He knows her longing for him, the depth of it, like he's lived it, like he's calling for his own mother, his own child, his own mate. It's the sound of remembering, of knowing all at once what you've lost. It's not all about Orrus. Not even close.

It ends, leaving his ears ringing, his mind obliterated, his heart heavy with loss. He raises his head, rubs his eyes clear. She stands a mere body length from him, the lamps of her eyes flaring. Her neck extends as far as it can toward him.

Her nose twitches as she tastes the air between them. She growls softly.

Growl is no longer the proper word.

"I know," he says. "I know." He shakes his head, mind emptied, can't hold any more.

"Help me," he says.

For a long moment she stands there, staring at him. He recognizes the look in her eyes a moment before she moves; he leaps at her but he's got no chance—she's already past him, and by the time he rises he's lost sight of her. But then he sees movement along the coastline and realizes she's headed south, toward home. He gives chase. He doesn't think, doesn't curse his slowness because it wastes breath. There's nothing left from the first chase; the dust is silent within him and he, the man, is exhausted. He trips, falls, collects cuts and bruises like any man will, clumsily running in the dark but running *hard*, unmindful of anything that may happen to him.

It's that she's so intent on putting distance between them. She's never done that before.

Fuck, a man is slow. Regardless, he's close enough to see their familiar stretch of beach. He sees it. He sees a dark streak upon it, a four-legged form running, stopping—digging? biting?

The dust. Orrus's box.

A star blooms upon the beach. The shockwave lifts him off his feet.

He finds her on a small, sandy ridge above the beach. Where she was thrown. He wastes two seconds staring at her, broken, chest barely rising, eyelights dimming. He slaps his hands on his thighs and roars, steam rising from his mouth like smoke into the gellid air. The tears freeze on his cheeks.

"Fucking *dog*!" he shouts, "Why you gotta be such a DOG!"

He turns, searching the beach for Orrus's box.

He finds it two hundred meters south of where she landed, laying in the center of a shallow bowl pressed into the sand. The sides of the bowl are smooth and hard, and directly under the box the sand has turned to glass. He says the words, to be sure it still opens. He keeps his thumb under the lid to be sure it doesn't close again and runs back to her.

He measures out a portion of dust—a gram, maybe a bit more; enough to resurrect and obliterate a man all at once. His hands are shaking. He stops a couple times, waiting for the black spots to clear from his vision.

He opens her jaws, holds her tongue down with one hand, and pours the dust down her throat. She chokes, coughs dust and blood in his face. He wipes off what he can and reaches into her mouth, wiping his fingers clean on the back of her tongue. She bites down on his wrist, but it's barely enough to call it a bite. Dosing. Dosing. What does it matter? He takes another gram or so, swishes it around his mouth as best he can, and spits it into her mouth.

"C'mon, girl," he says.

"Don't go," he says.

She opens her eyes, but the glow is dim. Her tongue is dry, far colder than usual. Her breathing is shallow but slow; her chest barely rises. He presses an ear against her chest, counting one heartbeat for every three of his. His hands rove over her long form, dismayed at the odd angles of her bones. A portion of her chest is caved in, her hip crushed. Her spine is intact, miraculously. He gets in close, peering into the fading light of her left eye. She whines, a sound so soft he wonders if he imagined it. He's stroking her ear, saying *please please please, come back, come back.*

Her whine ends in a soft exhalation. Her chest doesn't rise again. "Girl!" He shakes her. "No! Come! Come *back here*, now. NOW."

Her body convulses; she coughs blood into his face and lays still, smoke rising from her mouth.

"Sr—"

Her legs spasm straight; her front feet hit him in the chest, sending him flat onto his back in the sand. He scrambles up to find her convulsing, her body about to fall from the ridge. He tries to hold her back but he can't; he falls on his ass in the sand, arms wrapped around her. She stills and he listens. She convulses again, broken bones shifting under her fur, under his desperate hands as a buzzing builds within her, like bees stuck in a wall. Her lips peel back, bloodied teeth closed around a gurgling growl. Her eyes flash like an alchymical flare, once, twice, blinding him. Heat gathers so quickly inside her that he scrambles to get his legs out from beneath her. He crabwalks back.

She stands, her movements odd, puppet stiff. Her bones pop and click. As he watches, her back left leg—mangled, broken and folded back on itself—straightens and supports her. Her head snaps up and she howls, a jet of flame erupting from between her long jaws.

"Sroma!" he says. "Sroma!" He stamps his heels in the sand. "Sit! *Down!*"

Fool thing to say. Foolish thing, a man. She ignores him. She throws her head back and vomits a stream of fire into the night. Thick black smoke rises from her shoulders and back, animate, searching, coiling around the pillar of flame spearing the sky. Her body quivers, loses focus. The heat is incredible. He scoots backward. He runs.

Her mouth snaps shut like a handclap, snuffing out the flame as though it never existed. He stumbles in the sand, falls flat on his face. The heat diminishes enough for him to breathe. He turns but doesn't stand.

She's leveled her gaze on him. She steps forward and stops, sniffing the air between them. She advances slowly, head and tail low. She comes close enough to his face to lick or bite him. The stink is awful, a body burning. He stares into her eyes. She shows her teeth and growls deep in her chest. The vinegar-shit smell of her breath brings tears to his eyes but he doesn't move. His body shakes with tension; his fingernails bite gouges in his thighs.

"Girl," he says softly. *"Sit.* Sit now."

She huffs, blowing snot in his face. He flinches but keeps still.

Her growl shifts to a hoarser register. It stops. She arches her back and extends her neck forward, toward his chest. He thinks she's choking.

She throws up on him, soaking him in reeking, boiling vomit. He scampers back and rolls to the side, pressing his belly and chest to the cold sand. He thrashes until the vomit is off, the pain eased. He takes great big breaths, coughs, tries to catch his breath again. When he does catch it, he fills his lungs enough to think, to know he wants to hurt something, despite his exhaustion, despite it being *her*.

He growls. He gets up.

She sits as if posed for a portrait—head high, mouth closed, posture erect. She shows no sign of injury, no sign of any of it. She stares at him. He pauses, because he must admire her even now.

In this pause she barks, and in this bark is the command. His mind empties and he steps forward until she barks again.

He stares into her eyes. She looks down. He looks down.

A white egg. He blinks it into better focus. Clean—spotless. A border of dry sand surrounding it.

He reaches for it.

Kua, Semet al-E, Southern Ob, Iswee
(Fall—22 years old)

He rises from the bed slowly, breathing tight and fast because he's scared of how hurt he is, how fragile his body may be—not even when the girls beat him in the alley did he feel like this, not even the time Okin hit him and his head smacked the dining room table. *Don't get up*, his body tells him; wiser thing to do, stay still, let it do the work. But he can't be here any longer. He stands, swaying to get his balance right, and stares down at Dorone. The elderim is sealed in his armor, drugged on dust, curled into a ball like a baby, like a kitten.

Amur walks outside, where the world is too bright. He blinks at the sea, the western horizon. The sun nearly touches it, and for a moment he struggles to comprehend what it means.

It is the same day. Orrus died hours ago, only a comprehensible collection of seconds ago. He shakes his head and hobbles down the steps and down the bluff. He's not as injured as he imagined, perhaps.

The dust, he reminds himself. He freezes for a moment, listening to his body.

("Oh, you'll be fine," Dorone says, preparing their separate doses. "It's just a teensy bit, only a few grains." He leans against the kitchen counter; his movements are stiff but his muscles are oddly slack, as if the armor alone holds him upright. He offers Amur his dose and smiles handsomely, but the pain is written on his face. Amur stares at the glass. Dorone's hand begins to shake and water slops over its sides.

"Fucking take it, boy!")

He has to remind himself to unclench his fists, to stretch and breathe. The sand is cool under his feet. The breeze is clean, piercing. He holds a deep breath against the ache of his body. When he breathes out again, the pain is lessened. Repeat. After a while—seconds? minutes? doesn't matter—it's a distant thing.

"Holy *shit*," he says. He imagines what kind of damage Dorone has sustained, how close the elderim was to death. He thinks about killing Dorone—what it may take for a man so inclined. It will take more than a man. He chuckles at the idea, but he wants it, he does. He feels wounded, like a child, at the thought of never having such power. He feels angry at the thought of other people having such power.

The tide has gone out and the beach is broad and shiny. He avoids the pit of fused glass further up in the sand, all that remains of Orrus. He doesn't even look in the direction of the rock outcropping in the sand, the grey stones beyond which the Hound lies.

"Shielded her," he mumbles.

When his toes touch the water, he is suddenly afraid.

He feels fine. Regardless, he shuffles like an old, old man into the calm, warm surf. He continues until the water reaches his belly button. He stares at the sky. The moons rise. He tracks their movement across a section busy with stars: Berun, unwhole, wounded with a crater so massive he can fit Fyra inside himself. Fyra, smooth as a baby's cheek, sometimes far, sometimes near. She never touches him.

Once, they say, there were thirty moons. Before that, there was one. They say a lot of shit.

He loses sense of his body below the waterline. The fear returns; it feels like his feet are floating free of the bottom; but the sensation quickly passes. He won't be carried away. What a mad idea, Amur Ola drowning! When Dorone wakes from his immense, impossible wounds, Amur will still be here, bound to him.

Eventually, he exits the sea and sits, thinking nothing. The moons rise high into the starblown sky. When he does think again, he thinks clearly. He knows it's a bad decision.

He walks until he finds the Hound, curled like she's sleeping in the sand behind the grey rocks. The smell of wet fur, like a washrag left too long in the sink, fills his head. He doesn't give himself time to think. He breathes in, out, in, and holds. He squats and gets as much of her cold wet bulk in his arms and heaves, breathing out explosively, flopping her onto her other side. He shudders, eyes closed, heart trying to punch through his chest, as his body screams protest. He opens his eyes.

"Fuck," he says, staring at her. "Sorry." She's in an awful posture. He fights the urge to rearrange her, make her sleep again.

He looks down.

The Hound's soul is a cloudy red marble pulsing with light.

He holds it tenderly. It is warm to the touch. It is solid; it feels more like a lead bullet than a marble. He grips it in his fist. He's shaking, head to toe. He walks away and lays on the cold sand. His body aches. The Hound's soul disappears in his hand, he's gripped it long enough. He looks at his other hand and for one odd moment is tempted to lick it. He thinks of Marus. He imagines doing what Orrus asked, what he demanded, the entire thing. He imagines himself the owner of a dog. Perhaps he'll grow used to its presence. That awkward, over-eager body always following him, getting in his way.

His whole life, she'll be with him.

He tenses to throw her soul out to sea. He nearly does.

Judror, Kingdom of Casta Setjis
(Winter—35 years old)

He listens to his neighbor beat the dog for two nights. He stays out of other people's business; he does. But everyone has limits. Whiskey helps. When he can't listen to it any longer, he exits his flat and claps at his neighbor's door. It's raining and the awning's leaking on him. He is ignored, so he claps again, louder. The dog barks and is reprimanded with a shout.

"Nah want ya," the man says. "Shove off."

Amur claps twice more, loudly. He smiles at the creak of the man's chair, the stupid threats the man yells. His fingers curl into fists.

"Aw fuck no you *don't!*" the man shouts. Heavy footsteps, drunken cadence. Drunker than Amur, probably, not like it matters. The man comes right up to the door: "Back the fuck up, mate!"

Amur pictures the dude so clearly—spittle flying from his mouth as he shouts at a panel of wood. The kind of guy who gets in your face the second he feels small. The kind who buys friends to back him up, make sure he doesn't get too hurt.

Amur listens until the man backs away from the door.

"What I *said*, ya," the man says.

Amur chuckles and kicks the door near the handle, busting the lock from the frame. The door flies open.

"*Who the fuck're y—.*"

Amur steps in and knocks the man to the floor with a backhand slap.

Barking, stiff-legged: the dog in the corner is a larger, more capable looking thing than Amur imagined. He pictured it thin and mangy. Hackles raised, it growls and steps forward. Fear, not loyalty. Amur spreads his long arms and growls back. The dog pisses on the floor and keeps up the racket.

The man groans, staring up at Amur. More confused and scared than angry. He's pale and freckled, but not ugly as Amur guessed from the few glances he spared the man. Not long out of his teens, well built—only just starting to go fat around the middle. Green eyes. A thick lower lip. Not a hateful or angry face. Not yet. Amur looks around the place. Looks like shit, like his own did when he was the same age.

For a moment, Amur reconsiders. Parents probably gave him everything. Fucking fool *can't* know better.

His eyes land on the string of lavender prayer beads hung on a nail in the wall.

"Get up," he says.

The physician appraises Amur first, noting the quality of his clothes, the clarity of his skin, before shifting her gaze to the broken man slung over his shoulders. "It's late. I don't know exactly what I'm looking at here," she says. "He looks half dead. I should report this to some authority, probably."

Amur rolls his eyes. "Probably. How much to heal him?"

She shrugs, sucking loudly at her front teeth. She extends a chymical-stained hand to catch a drop of blood as it drips from the tip of the man's nose. She's beautiful, thick and vital. She's got two lavender bangles on each forearm, so he hates her. It occurs to him that he has enough dust, more than the physician will see in her lifetime, to heal the man. More likely to kill him. Still, he's tempted.

fuck, fuck fuck, fuck fuck, he says under his breath. Of course it's begun to rain.

"For half dead?" she says. "Twelve hundred, at least."

A ridiculous amount. Far beyond what he imagined. What does it matter? He doesn't need her just for the healing. "Can you…?"

"I can make him forget who did this. Expensive."

He nods. She gestures him in.

Mssrs Adonbe & Shaume,

As of this morning, 13-10-213, I have absented my premises at 3 Herring #2, Rareale. I have enclosed banknotes for the remainder of my rent, through Financiers '214, as required per my lease. I am contracting with Espers for the transfer of my personal effects as well as the cleaning of the apartment. They will contact you shortly for access.

- Amur Ola

He puts the pen down. He stares at the letter, eyes unfocused, mind emptied. Out the eastern window, his gaze lands on the domed roofs of the Isweean Consulate. He shutters the window. He picks up the statue of Vedas, moves his fingertips over its familiar angles. There's a circle of dust where the statue sat. He hasn't moved much in the apartment since the breakup. He puts the statue back down.

There's not a thing Fyen hasn't touched, didn't touch. The stained leather armchair, maybe. ("That thing is disgusting. "That quirk of the eyebrow when he can't figure Amur out. "You sit in it, naked, after your fucking sweaty-ass exercise! That's just gross, love.") No, Fyen wasn't fond of the chair.

He starts thinking about it hard, like he's done endless times before; maybe it *can* be salvaged. What's four months apart?

"Nope," he says. "Nope, nope, nope." He drops to the floor, forces out fifty clap-pushups. By the fortieth, his arms are shaking and his brand new beer gut is slapping the floor. He half squats and holds the posture until his legs threaten to fall out beneath him.

He retrieves the old Salwan field bag and wood-framed rucksack from the closet. The familiar textures, the baked-in smell of smoke and sun, the dull honey scent of beeswax. Once, he wasn't afraid to set off. After Dorone, he couldn't wait to get out of Nos Min. He pedaled for months, east across the Continent, through the Five Nations. He was daring, he supposed.

He remembers the road, packed with traffic—single travelers on pannier-laden touring bikes, thick-thighed hauling teams on their massive multi-wheeled cycles, the rare elderim in a dust-propelled carriage. The smell of rubber and cement, stone and dirt; the taste of road-grit every time he licked his lips. The world passing him by. Strangers packed into roadside hostels. He remembers his fear, of being robbed, of being raped, of everything he'd ever heard would happen outside Nos Min. He remembers how he couldn't let it go, Dorone's cruelty at their parting; he thought of it a hundred times each day, pedaling, pedaling. He watched the sky like Dorone would descend out of it. He must have opened the field bag a dozen times each day, confirming that the soul and the dust were still there. He didn't dare open the box, even when he was completely alone.

Squatting, he presses on the hidden panel under his desk. The drawer pops open. He lifts the circle of catgut over his head, returns the locket to his chest. It's heavier than he remembers. It always is. Hand held to his chest, the familiar heat of her against his skin.

"Sorry," he says. It feels insufficient.

He grabs Orrus's enchanted box of dust and rises, straight-backed but lost. He traces the lines of script on the box, which feels like firm leather but resists any mark or scratch. True Elderskin, he suspects—itself nearly priceless. He holds it like he's holding a wounded animal, like he's holding a bomb. He can't see the wards protecting it, but he believes in their potency. He whispers the Elder words, and the lid clicks open. He opens the box and stares at the neat packets of white dust, pure Elder bone from Iswee itself, nothing like what they mine from Noerre.

Among men, he can do almost anything. What he wants can't be bought.

He grips the locket in his fist.

"Help," he whispers to her.

He wakes before dawn, after only two hours of sleep. He tromps down the steps of his stoop, his pannier-packed bike over his shoulder, his rucksack on his back. He pedals off without a backward glance. The weather's shit, it's cold, but at least no rain. Yet.

In his packs, panniers, and rear cargo trailer:

Three waterproofed down quilts; four slings and 500 clay bullets; a composite recurve bow and two sheaves of arrows; a hatchet; a creaky Castan Infantry folding cot and frame tent canopy; a toiletry kit; a stubby rainbow-swirled hash pipe; fifteen trashy paperbacks; a sheaf of banknotes; a legal notice, dated 15,205, informing him that he'd been written out of his mothers' will; and the leather portfolio containing Dorone's letters. Orrus's dust, of course.

At the last moment, he recalls the animal repellent he bought half a decade ago. He was going back, he told himself then. He *was*. Back home. He planned it all out: Same route. Same places. Different man.

At Espers, the consultant informs him the contents of his apartment will arrive in Bosqu, a city in the northwestern corner of Toma near the Nosi border, by the tail end of Spring. Amur has never been there, but it's dry and it's on the sea. He pays more to have the contents stored on arrival for a few months. He worries about his records most. His art, his music journals. The armchair. A lot can happen crossing the Continent.

He won't be taking the trade routes again, but the blessed road of the Return. Up the Steps, over the roof of the world, following Vedas's path. Signing the paperwork at Esper's, he starts to get anxious.

Less than two kilometers from his neighborhood and he's winded, itchy with sweat. His belly jiggles. His shoulders chafe against the pack straps; his inner thighs chafe against the bike seat. Teeth clenched until his jaw aches, he pedals to the southern border of the city, cursing himself for his insistence on a weight-saving three-speed. "Your legs adapt," he told Fyen. So much for that; he hasn't ridden the damn thing in a year, at least.

Of Judror's neighborhoods, the southernmost, Lusces, most reminds him of home. The crumbling, close-packed tenements are the wrong color, the wrong shape, but the smells are fuller than in the rest of the city, the clothing prettier and more practical. They do normal people things—plant fruit trees along sidewalks, let children run loose all day, stretch laundry lines from window to window rather than use separate musty rooms for drying.

Of course, there are more Nosi here. More Tomen, too, as well as Ulome and some native Castans. Amur hasn't been here in months, not since Fyen.

("You don't like it here," Fyen says of their place in Rareale. They've been here a year. "I mean, I don't like it either. Area's changing too fast. We could always move somewhere else. Maybe you'd feel more at home in Lusces."

Amur feels it—the future coming up to hit him. He doesn't need to let it upset him.

"What did you just say to me? More at *home*?")

Now, as he always does, he wonders why he stayed away. And, as always, the answer is obvious: *Whoa, who gave you that hair? What's your name? No, your* last *name. Uh-huh. And where you say you're from? Where you live* now*?* He's paranoid—like they can just look at him and know his story. Man who got dragged away by the prince himself!

It's a weird thing, avoiding your own people.

The Return is no longer a common practice, even among the descendents of Vedas. Nowadays, only two types of Nosi set upon the Return: zealots and rich old men. Both groups pass through Lusces on their journey, north to Doreth Lum or south to the Steps and across the Continent. Amur is neither a stick-thin ascetic nor an oiled and bejeweled ancient upon a painted pedicab powered by four huge men, at the head of a train of porters and guards.

So folks *stare* as he pedals by. He doesn't mind; the looks are mostly friendly. He stays silent except when he's returning the blessing.

"Be with you."

"With you."

He buys hardtack, jerky, raisins, dried herbs, four canteens, sixteen pints of cold-sealed beer, water purification tablets, and twenty grams of weed flower, filling up the space in the trailer. A handsome trader talks him into a friction-generator headlamp for his bike—an item so expensive, so indulgent and *modern*, that he packs it away with everything else rather than affixing it to the frame.

Those who overcharge him, he pays without argument. Those who charge fairly, he pays as if they've asked for more. He buys cheap candy from kids and hands it out to other kids. Some of the richer travelers on the Return do this sort of thing. Richer folks have guards. A few people size him up but wisely keep back. There's muscle shifting under that gut. Look at those shoulders! A few guys do give him the eye, and he ignores it, and the guys don't try anything.

"Yo!" someone calls when he's nearly out of town. "You maybe got something?"

Amur tries not to stare, and then he simply stares.

A Coumeng, appaloosa patterned white and tan. They's on crutches and they's got no left leg. A veteran, by the look of the tattoos crisscrossing their sinuous arms and hands. Their home is more shack than house, and a few empty lots separate it from the closest tenements. It looks tidy and secure, though.

He doesn't know shit about Coumeng, not one bit. Some good music drifts out the open window—a loud low beat and throbbing bass, a wiry riff winding over it. The singing is sleazy and dangerous sounding. The Coumeng watches him standing there, listening to it.

"Institute," they says. "Heard 'em?"

Amur shakes his head and flips them 20j—next to nothing, but they smiles like it's a good haul. "Be with you," they says.

Amur frowns. It wasn't a test or anything, to see if they was grateful. He wants to leave them something. He looks north up the avenue; there are more than a few eyes watching them. He turns back south.

"See that half-burnt stump a little ways up?" he says softly.

"Yup," they says.

When Amur reaches the burnt mesquite, he drops his coin pouch on his right foot and lets it tumble to the ground. There's more than a few big coins in there, maybe even a 50u, which will present a problem. That's a big, big coin. It draws attention. Good problem to have, ultimately; the Coumeng looked like they could handle themself.

Another kilometer of riding brings him to the edge of the Epal Rim, a tall limestone escarpment separating northern and southern Casta Setjis. Below him is a sea of green, an expanse of forest reaching nearly to the horizon. (He's never been too good with trees; there are *lots of trees*. Ylm, he imagines. Oak? None of those dry scraggly pine like back home.) The grey-brown line of the Return, visible here and there through the verdance, follows a snaking path south through the forest. Red, rounded mountains crouch on the horizon, where it's also raining. Of course it's raining.

He turns and acknowledges the dog. It's followed him, the whole way through the city, keeping well back until now.

"I didn't do it for *you*," he says. "I just didn't want to listen to it anymore."

The dog cocks its head. It lowers its muzzle, wags its tail tentatively, and takes two steps closer. Amur hooks his thumb over the strap of his pack. He has enough jerky and water purification tablets for two; hell, he's got enough for *five*. He knows how to hunt even if he's shit at what kind of tree the fucking squirrel's in.

He thinks of Agra. She cried the first time she killed a squirrel. Amur's fault that she was even out hunting. She was good at it, though. She liked animals more than him, always had. He never thinks about that. He doesn't think about her often at all. He thinks of Chora even less. Chora wouldn't *ever* let a creature with four legs in the house.

He closes his eyes, breathes into his gut, and drops his hand.

"You got family out there, but they're nothing like you. They'll rip you apart."

He turns to face the wilderness again. The dog follows. Only a kilometer or two down the switchback path into the forests of southern Casta Setjis, however, it stops in place and barks, refusing to follow him any further.

•

A decade in Judror, a place as removed from Jalast as Continental geography allows—does he think himself a different man? He stares at the fire and considers it. It's an old dialogue, going nowhere. Nonetheless, he adds up what he's done, what he hasn't, and draws the inescapable conclusion, the same conclusion he always draws:

He squandered his time, not because he didn't live it but because he was always somewhere else, some*when* else, young and naive and hurt. The drama of it all! How he held himself, like he was hoping not to be noticed when he wanted so badly to be noticed, but not like he was always noticed—no, he was looking for something different, but fuck if he could tell you what it was. He walked, shoulders in, head down, even when he wasn't thinking of Dorone. When he roused pride, it was a put-on; it was arrogance, just another sort of fear.

Or maybe it wasn't so bad. Depends on how he looks at it. He peers down at the locket.

"Most of the time, it was horrible," he says.

The river burbles behind him. (*R. Awp*, says a labeled Return map he acquired from a teenage Nosi who looked like she didn't give a damn if he bought it from her mothers' shop. He admired her disdain, relishing in the fact that she didn't give a shit who he was, what he looked like.) He slaps mosquitos and noseeums. Always, the fucking bugs in this place! Why's he lived here so long? It *is* admittedly worse here than in the city. Surrounded by trees. Hemmed in. And to think of how comfortable he was only a day or two ago. From the second floor he had a view of the sea. He had to peer just so between the buildings, and it was often obscured by fog, but still. He could have afforded more; he can always afford more.

(He's leaving, he's finally got the courage, and he's said it all in one big rush, ending here, on the most pathetic part:

"I still expect to be paid."

Dorone stares at him and for a moment Amur thinks he's going to die. Dorone is going to kill him. But the elderim's speech is quiet and precise, a knife in Amur's gut:

"Oh, you'll be paid. I'll be so generous you'll never be able to think of anything else.")

Across the fire sits his rucksack. He stares at it like it's an old enemy. He thinks of Okin, the way she was, how horrible it was to live under the thumb of someone who hates you fundamentally, for reasons you can't hope to change. He thinks of Dorone, and the way someone can just lie so openly, with such nonchalance—for deception to be as much a part of you as throwing parties and killing old friends.

He sees Orrus kneeling over the Hound's body. Orrus leaking light from his eyes.

He hasn't read any of Dorone's letters in years. He doesn't *want* to think about Dorone. It's an obligation, somehow, like paying bills or checking the door a couple times to see if it's really locked. He looks at his mothers' notice of separation now and then, hating it because it's the only thing he's got of them and it's nothing Chora would have chosen. Chora only follows along because that's what you do; you follow along or you get hurt. While he's thinking of his mom he thinks of Agra. He wonders how she is, who she's making feel like a fool. He'll go home someday.

A wild dog howls, followed by a packmate. A third, a fourth, join in. Closer than he likes. There's not much to hide in or on; so far the Awp is too shallow to seek much refuge in, and the trunks of the trees along its banks are too high to climb. He decides not to worry about it because there's no point.

For once, reasoning it out works. And he has the repellent. He imagines walking into the night and just letting the dogs take him. What a stupid thing to think about.

He smokes a bowl, knowing it'll make him more worried about the dogs. He thinks about the dog that followed him through the city, about how he could have allowed it along. He thinks about how much worry it would have caused. Thing can't always be on a lead. He imagines it here, right now, the moment when it's heard too much of that wild yapping and runs off into the night—leaving him alone, staring into the darkness, knowing the dog stands no chance against its wild cousins.

He's never known much about dogs. Too busy being Amur, the pretty boy, the boy who got everything his way. Then being home, doing all *that* shit. He doesn't like dogs.

His gaze returns to the rucksack. He sighs loudly, like he's about to speak and maybe he was. Instead he spits into the fire, stands with a groan of stiff muscle, and reaches across the flames for the rucksack. As he brings it close, he lets its bottom linger in the fire. The smell of heated canvas, a hint of burn. He pulls out his mothers' letter and the portfolio.

He stares down at his chest, brows creased. His fingertips brush the locket. His locket. Without putting down the paperwork, he grabs a pint of beer and twists it open. Alchymicals fizz; frost moves up the bottle, under his fingers. He stares into the fire. He drinks half the beer before the hand holding the paperwork stops shaking.

He doesn't know why he does it, but he knows he'll regret it and does it anyway. A simple flick of the wrist.

Prota, Medile Sea
(Fall—43 years old)

It was easy to acquire. He hopes they didn't kill it; they told him it drowned in the storm. Now it's here, on the floor. Black, like he envisioned. He considers it a moment, then considers the luminous marble in his palm.

He places Sroma's soul next to its nose. He takes a sixteenth-gram of dust—a guess, based on nothing, really—and pours it carefully down its tiny throat. He stares at it, here on the floor like it's sleeping.

"Fuck," he says.

His fingers find the bottle. He downs the laced beer in three gulps. His mouth is filled with the taste of copper, of blood. He counts heartbeats… 25. 50. 100. Nothing comes—no waves crashing in his skull, no blades of light splitting his mind into mirror twins of itself. His heart moves heavily, resolutely. The dust is new to him, and unpredictable, but it certainly hasn't summoned resolve.

He stares at it. He feels like a child, afraid of a big bug.

He uncorks a second beer, this one unlaced, and drinks half. The lip of the bottle is salty from his hand. He stares at his hand for a moment, keeping unwelcome thoughts at bay. He thinks of Chora, and how much she hated animals in the house. He thinks of Agra, but it's harder to focus on her right now. She loved animals; she couldn't understand *why-oh-why* they couldn't have a dog. She wanted a dog.

He breathes deep into his belly.

"Okay," he says. "Enough. It's not complicated."

He pushes Sroma's soul into its mouth and waits. He sits down and watches.

The body twitches and he flinches. The skin under its coat squirms and he stands. The muscles in his thighs jump. He wants to run. He wants to stamp it out, stop this from happening. A hiss comes from it, like air escaping a bladder, comes from it. The sound becomes a long exhalation, which stops suddenly and turns into an inhalation. The breaths shorten. The body whines. Its back leg kicks. He flinches again, and laughs at himself.

He kneels. He doesn't reach out to touch it. Not yet.

It becomes a puppy, alive, blind and whimpering on the floor.

—elsewhere—

The cabin is gone. She is gone. He is gone.

He is standing on firm feet, alone. He feels fine. He turns a full circle. A field of blue and pink flowers extends in all directions; they are under his feet, crumpled, spiky-soft in a way he likes. He wants to examine them but does not. There are no hills, no trees, no buildings. The horizon is wrong. It does not bend in a distant arc but seems to simply fade out in a massive circle, to become sky, the same no matter which way he turns. It is impossible to determine how far away the end is, if it is an end at all. Maybe he can walk this carpet of blue and pink forever, reaching nowhere. It is neither night nor day. There is a slight breeze at his back at all times, any direction he turns. When he recognizes this fact, a breeze, he inhales cautiously and then deeply through his nose. He is filled with the scent of the flower, pleasant and clean, a citrus aroma like jesamine. It leaves him clear headed and eager. He stretches his limbs, flexes his mucles like a kid. He finds it normal, being so hale and sound. He gazes into the sky. There is no sun, no moons, only a ceiling of stars. Densely packed. Close. Lifting his right hand, he is surprised to find that it does not encounter resistance or heat. He cannot bat the stars aside. His eyes are fooled by this place, perhaps, and he cannot see how far from him they are. "Disappointing," he says. He flinches at the sound and then at the idea. Of speaking here. His voice is flat, quieter than he anticipated. He repeats the word, and it makes him feel, again: He should not be talking. And the word knows it, stopping the moment it leaves his mouth. He is naked, unadorned but for a white egg shape stamped upon his chest, its surface smoother than flesh, the union so absolute he cannot insert a fingernail under it or pry its edge up. The symbol is significant, yet focusing his mind on it proves difficult. Why think about it? It is supposed to be here, upon him, within him. This, he knows for certain. He stares at it, expecting something, but not sure what. Not even a clue.

A breeze against his chest. He looks up. Two men are walking toward him.

They are naked, black skinned, strongly built. They may be brothers, or father and son. They may be his own ancestors. They are beautiful like few men are. They stand closer to each other than to Amur.

The one on Amur's left is the taller. His skin is black, no shading of brown. No hair, no scars or tattoos, mar his broad-shouldered perfection. HIs body is that of an elite athlete, a wrestler or acrobat or both. His face is handsome, masculine and graceful, mature yet smooth like stone. His penis is large but not unusually so. His eyes are a radiant white, lacking iris. He meets Amur's gaze without expression and Amur must look away.

The man to the right does not look at Amur or the other man. He stares into the distance as if there is something to see. His body is nearly as beautiful as the other man's, but it is fully a man's body, not a god's. He is dark, perhaps not as dark as Amur, and he is hairless but for salt-and-pepper pubic hair and eyebrows. He has scars. It is obvious he has fought and lived. His face, too, is beautiful, with high cheekbones and full lips, lined from exposure and expression. An old injury causes him to lean slightly, to hold one shoulder higher than the other.

Amur returns his gaze to the first man, who raises a white brow in query.

"Who—" Amur.

"Shut up," the second, imperfect man says. His voice is deep and clear—*close*, as though he is standing nose to nose with Amur. "Only I speak. This is a sacred place, Amur Ola. Respect it."

Now he turns his head and meets Amur's gaze. Amur's heart beats faster, staring into the man's eyes, a golden-brown so rich they are nearly alight. He wants to touch this man, to close his eyes and run his fingers over his face, run his hands over the course of his scarred body. He wants to ask questions, and it does not matter what questions. He wants to hear the man talk again. *Say anything, man.*

The other man, the perfect one, chuckles and crouches, capturing Amur's attention. He runs his hand over the carpet of blue and pink flowers. He grips a handful of stems and pulls them out of the ground. He smells the flowers, all of them pink and vibrant, glowing as if bathed in sunlight, and then drops them with an indifferent toss of his hand. Sighing, he stares up at Amur, and Amur is transfixed by his beauty. Amur stares at the man's body, his cock. He becomes aware of his own body again, his own desire.

"This one," the second man says, and Amur knows by the sounds of his voice that he dislikes, maybe even hates, the other man, the very beautiful one. Amur can't look away from the crouching man, the very beautiful one. "He has things to tell you. It won't be here."

The corners of the couching man's lips turn up slightly, and his eyes take on a golden hue. Light pours from his eyes, so that Amur is filled with light, golden and ringing like a singing bowl. The man closes his eyes. Amur closes his eyes.

The world becomes warm, perfect, before it goes out.

They came from the forest at their backs. This is all he knows about it. They are walking an overgrown stone path toward the sharp edge of a cliff. The grassland around them is vast and flat, tilted slightly toward the cliff, and beyond it—far, far beyond and below—is the bluegreen expanse of the sea.

The grasses are in wild bloom, a beautiful mess of green and blue and pink. It is an easy walk, not a short walk, and the air is lively and full of spring smells. The sky is bright, cloudless. They are moving south, the sun descending on the right, shadows lengthening on the left. They walk for some time, not speaking.

He regards his companion. The man is resplendent, clothed in ankle-length skirts that shift through shades of red, tiny golden bells along the hems chiming softly. He wears clunky, wood-bead bracelets and ivory rings. His upper chest and shoulders are speckled with color—small and large spots in rainbow hues. A golden band rests low on his crown, molded to the shape of his skull.

Amur stops to examine himself. He is accoutred identically but in a different palette: skirts in shades of yellow (of fabric so luxuriously smooth he simply stands for a time, rubbing it between his fingers), chest and shoulders speckled in white and gold—dye, perhaps, as the texture is no different from his own skin. He wears the same jewelry as the other man, though his crown is of wood and stone, ingeniously carved as though woven together, a braid of flax and slate.

Something catches his eye in the grass. He crouches to look:

A bracelet of stone beads, a shade of pink so bright it seems to glow. Brighter, even, than the blooming grasses. He places it on his left wrist.

His companion hasn't stopped. Amur jogs to catch up, filled with the smell of the place. Grasses, dirt, occasionally some sort of pine, only occasionally the sea. Not the smell of home, but something he knows.

"Up the steps," he says, confused but uncaring. "Blessed path."

He whispers, like there's a rule he's breaking. He grins like a kid.

He rejoins the other man. Soon they step from the overgrown path onto a still white surface, softly rippled and scalloped like the bed of a shallow stream. Soon, its surface extends all around them, a vast petrified lake, and for a moment he's afraid. This is one of those old types of stories—Little Vedas is about to open his eyes for real and sink into that lake, and the lake's gonna close over his head, trap him forever.

A hand on his upper arm, fingers encircling his wrist.

"You're fine," a voice says.

He smiles and nods at the beautiful man who stands before him, who is so like him, this kind brother or cousin or uncle. He nods in agreement, smiling with all his teeth. "Yeah, yeah. I'm cool, I'm cool," he says, unbothered by the man's frown. He shrugs and starts walking again, admiring the surface under his feet. No dirt collects in its scalloped shadows, and walking on it is lovely. When Amur closes his eyes, he convinces himself it is shifting underfoot, like sand. A stroll on the beach. He frowns and then smiles, forgetting whatever made him frown. He's content to keep walking. The edge is so far away.

And then it is not. He is standing only a stone's throw from the cliff's edge, the wind blowing steadily at his back. He wants to look behind him, to see how far they've come, but for some reason he doesn't.

He and his companion have stopped before a low wall of grey stone. The wall extends in a half circle ten meters across, enclosing a small section of the plain against the cliff edge. The floor within the enclosure is black sand, shimmering kaleidoscopically in the angled light of the descending sun. There is no wall at the cliff's edge, and so a constant stream of sand flows over the edge, like water or smoke or silk streamers, twisting and whipping and dissipating.

It'll be gone before long at this rate, Amur thinks.

"This place was called Ghavur juh Yesa," the man says without turning. His voice is deep, mellifluous. The rainbow colors on his chest and shoulders glow; they rise from his skin and wink, in and out, to the rhythm of his speech. "An Elder word, it means something like *Youngest Sibling's Womb*." He furrows his brows. "I don't understand this now. I need what's inside to know that." The colors descend.

"Inside," Amur says. He shakes his head, staring down at his chest, at the white and gold spots rising from his skin. There is a larger oval of white upon his chest that does not move. "Okay," he says again, watching the rest of the spots tremble and rise. "Okay, okay, okay, okay…" They dance for him, to the sounds he makes.

The other man frowns, and steps over the wall. When his foot touches the black sand, he disappears. Amur's eyes widen. He peers around, unworried, like the man has performed a novel trick.

"Now?" Amur shakes his head. "Where…" He laughs out loud, waving his hands through the spots of white and gold, causing them to scatter, and steps over the wall.

Night has descended. The ground beneath him is soft, blacker than black, a void; it feels like he's standing in the sea, in the sky. He can no longer tell where the cliff ends. One moon, greywhite and whole, hangs like an eye over the water. He understands how far down the sea is, and whistles appreciatively.

"Where," he says again, and for a moment does not know who he is speaking to. The word, too, is confusing. He knows this place. "When," he says, and smiles: this feels like a better word. "When," he says again, watching the white and gold spots rise from his skin. "People," he says, and feels odd. He's said something foolish, out of place. He says it again, just to be sure. "People." He breathes in, deep into his belly. "People." He turns to the other man.

"Tell me. When. And people."

The man is standing before a pedestal of white stone topped with a broad, shallow bowl. He's removing his bracelets, his rings. He saves the crown for last, lifting it free slowly, methodically, as if it weighs a great deal. Regardless, once he's removed it he flings it to the side, out of sight.

"Longer ago than you can imagine. And there are no people here. Not anymore." The set of his shoulders changes; the brilliant spots above them dim. "Or not yet. Depends on what you mean by *people*. Come here, boy."

:*Don't call me boy*:

Amur blinks, dumbfounded by the new sound-not-sound he's made.

So simple—just speak, don't open your mouth. He smiles and the smile is also new, a man's smile, full of knowing. His fingers curl into fists. The spots of white and gold flare to life, white-hot embers rising from his chest and shoulders until they hang suspended above him, an umbrella of stars.

He knows where he is, roughly, what region of the world. He was here once, when he was young. Younger. But he was no boy, not even then. He'd made mistakes.

:My name is Amureru: he says with his new voice. He breathes calm into his limbs and flexes his hands like he's about to wrestle. The stars fall and adhere to him so that his arms and shoulders are dappled in light, his face freckled with stardust. *:You may call me Amur:*

The other man still doesn't turn. He sighs, however, and in some way it diminishes him.

"I have something for you, Amurereru Ola."

Amur joins the man, who is staring into the bowl atop the pedestal. Formed of clear glass or crystal, the broad, shallow bowl is bisected by a ridge running down its middle. Both depressions are filled with water. In the left is a white, four-fingered glove. In the right is a long, black knife.

The man places his hand above the water, over the submerged glove. "I don't yet know this is a choice, irrevocable, setting me on my path. I select the glove, and I assume the armor. I choose an extension of my will, not a companion to it. " He regards Amur. He looks him up and down, as if noticing his dress for the first time. He nods, grunting as though satisfied but only just. "Who made such relics, for what purpose, I'll never know. The armor itself doesn't know. Why would they just leave it here for me, for anyone to take? Do they not know I am here, that my people are only waiting?"

Amur stares at the knife. He touches his cheek. Waiting.

:What waiting, why?: he says.

The other man grimaces. "Me." He casts his gaze heavenward, eyes filled with moonlight. "I've lost heart. I've forgotten how to do what I am made to do." He looks back down at his hand, poised over the glove. "I am capable, in and of myself. But this—this will give me the resolve to wake men from their slumber, to take responsibility over them. The Elder will pass away, ceding this world to men, to the elderim."

Amur stares at the man until he meets Amur's gaze.

:Adrash:

"A fragment." The god again frowns. It seems all he does is frown. (Amur recalls him crouched, holding pink flowers, smiling up at him—where is that man now?) "I exist here, within the armor."

Adrash slips his hand into the water but stops short of touching the glove. He shakes his head and reaches instead into the second depression, taking hold of the knife. Wincing, he lifts it free of its bath and turns to Amur. Amur tenses but Adrash only flips the knife, catches it along the edge, and holds it out. Amur stares, transfixed, at its sleek black length.

"Take it," Adrash says through gritted teeth. Blood drips from his palm and disappears into the black sand.

Amur takes it and gasps as the blade seems to vibrate in his hand. Adrash steps forward and grips Amur's fingers tightly around the handle. The move has taken the god within Amur's guard; Adrash leans in close, until his mouth is inches from Amur's ear.

"Yes, it is. Ancient beyond reason, but alive. And you recognize it."

Amur knows this is true; there is something comforting about holding the blade. He wipes at his cheek, which has grown hot, and shakes the liquid from his hand. There is no liquid on his hand. Why would there be?

The thing speaks no words. Regardless, it's *here*—behind Amur's eyes, staring out, measuring. When he looks at Adrash, the god is no longer naked but sealed in white, encased head to toe in the seamless embrace of his armor, *the* armor. Amur presses his hand to Adrash's chest. The texture of the armor is smoother, colder than skin. He reluctantly takes his hand back, fingertips trailing on Adrash's pectoral.

The knife shivers in his grip. A low sound, a rumble,

builds—a growl from his own throat, he soon realizes, and stops himself.

Adrash releases his grip and steps back. The illusion of his armor fades. Amur stares down at his own chest, the white egg positioned in the center, fuzed to him. He traces a fingertip over it and smiles. He holds up the knife, squinting at it as though its beauty is blinding. He likes the way it feels in his hand.

"So. They will allow the other's touch," Adrash says. He holds his hand over the glove again. Amur watches a bead of blood fall into the water. The glove undulates like a jelly, growing a fifth finger. "I wasn't *allowed* to take possession of both. Too much for me." He closes his fist, squeezing a few more drops of blood into the water. "*Me.*"

Amur stares at him, his thoughts again scrambled.

:Possession: he says. *:Own. Ownership. No owning.:*

The god ignores him. "But a stonecutter's son who's done nothing of value, whose brain is already half rotted? *He*, you find worthy." He stares into the bowls. He pushes away from the pedestal and takes a few steps away from Amur. The light of his eyes doubles, trebles. "Your being *offends* me."

Amur shakes his head and submerges the knife. Slowly, finger by finger, he loosens his grip. Instantly, his mind clears. He presses his hand to his chest, to the relic, the armor, aware of its expansion inside him. With this gift, he needs nothing.

All the same, he reaches for the knife again. He wants to hold it, bend it to his will, and—he looks at Adrash—*stick it in this one's guts.*

He stops himself, which proves a challenge. He nods, as if the difficulty means something. He tears his gaze away from the knife and meets Adrash's eye. This god, this memory of a creature in the shape of a man who crippled the moon and held the world in his grasp, has no power over Amur other than knowledge, and even that... In time, Amur will know every one of the armor's secrets.

"What is it called?" he asks, even as the answer fizzes in the folds of his brain.

"Sroma," the god answers.

The second man sits in a rocking chair across the porch from him. It's a cool, humid night. The crickets are singing under an overcast sky.

Amur stands from the other rocking chair and walks beyond the perimeter of the front yard. A dirt road disappears into the darkness before him. He turns back to the house, which is straight-beamed but modest, probably only the one bedroom. Its interior is lit by an oil lamp in the glass window. There are neighbors—he sees other homes, other lights, far off—but the sense of isolation is intense, purposeful.

He's clothed only in loose white cotton pants. The armor is a stamp upon his chest. The ground is cold under his naked feet. The air smells like good Nosi dirt soaked with monsoon rain. They *are* in northern Nos Min, he knows at once—near Danoor. Home country. He fills his lungs, and for a moment he thinks he'll start walking and keep walking until he's there, in Jalast. Someone will be happy to see him. May take some convincing, but he's always been a charmer.

He returns to the porch and stands before the man, who is also half clothed in brown cotton pants. He's younger than before, with a few weeks worth of growth on his head and face. There's a fair bit of grey in his beard and temples, and it suits him. For a good while Amur is content to stare at the beautiful man, who is looking down at a cat's cradle splayed between his fingers.

When the man looks up, he doesn't look at Amur.

"My wife is dead," the man says. "Just happened. My son doesn't know it yet. I don't know it yet." He bares his teeth; not a smile. "In *life*, I don't know this yet. She was away. Heart just fucking stopped." The cat's cradle collapses into his fists.

Amur opens his mouth, closes it. He returns to the other chair—the man's wife's, he assumes. He stands, unsure.

"Who are you?" he asks.

The man looks back down at his hands. "An ancestor—a poor one, by the looks of you." He drops the strings on the porch. "Then again, if I'd been living *like* you... You crazy bastard. From now on, though, there's no need for any of that. No need for a lot of things. I have something to show you. If Churls were here, she would've done it already. Words exhaust her. They have since we lost Fyra. She was—" He closes his eyes, breathes out, breathes in.

Amur opens his mouth; he's going to say *sorry* or some such idiot thing. The man looks up, meeting Amur's gaze for the first time, and Amur is transfixed, awareness expanding. Pressure builds behind his eyes, pulsing, *daa-da, daa-da*—two syllables of insistence, a drumbeat, a heartbeat.

:Vedas: he says, realization flooding him. Heat rises to his cheeks. He kneels at the man's feet, feeling like a fool.

The man nods minutely and looks past Amur again, down the road and away. He turns in his seat, peering over his shoulder into the window behind him, the single lamp burning.

"Just fucking stopped—game over. Can you believe that."

Amur hears what the man says. He feels the man's pain. He's aware of his own compassion and curiosity, and he just listens. Someone raised him well.

:Chora: he says.

Vedas stands abruptly, descends the stairs and rounds the eastern corner of the house. Amur pauses a moment, caught by the urge to go into the house and look in on the man's son. Just to see if he'll be there, if the armor accounts even for that. He presses his hand to the front door. Instead, he follows Vedas around the house.

Amur smiles suddenly, like it's pulled from him. "Agra," he says, and smiles bigger. He breathes the monsoon in, the aroma of soaked dirt. The *best* smell.

The back of the property extends a fair way to a shallow, sycamore-lined arroyo, and beyond that stretches an expanse of desert. It's a lovely spot, managed so that the appearance of wilderness remains. Three large, flat stones sit equidistantly around a firepit under the canopy of a tall mesquite.

Vedas stands on the opposite side of the tree, staring up into its branches, which always look dingy this time of year as the leaves grow dry and brittle, ready to fall despite the rain, the life blooming all around.

Amur joins him. They stand as close as brothers, together peering into the tree. He's always been bad at trees, but this one's easy.

He thinks before he speaks. He wants to speak like a man.

"Once, when I was young, I stood under a mesquite like this." He shakes his head; this isn't what he meant to say. He can't recall what he meant to say. "It must've been just the right conditions—windy, with the pods all about to drop. They came down all at once, on me, and I stood there like it was raining."

"Odd rain," Vedas says. His voice is gentler than before.

Amur reaches up to find tears on his cheeks. He thinks of a boy and a dog, somewhere, anywhere. What an odd thought right now. He laughs, remembering. "Like having a pile of tiny sticks fall on you."

Vedas grunts. A nice sound. "You're not much like others, are you?"

Amur frowns. "What does that mean? I've been away, a long time."

"That's not what I meant. I didn't spend most of my life here either."

"What?"—and he means it. *What*? He's lost track again.

Vedas chuckles and Amur stares at him, full of nameless longing. They meet eyes and Amur knows it: this man has been here before, where Amur is, mind and body filled to incomprehension with newness. If only he can be allowed to pause and gather his bearings—may be days, may be a thousand years.

"I grew up here," Amur says. "Near here. Smells the same. Is… is what I've been thinking, is what this is, is it true?" He groans, holding his head in his hands.

Vedas grips his shoulder. He massages it the way men do, wincingly hard, and Amur feels as though he'll melt into the ground or be hurled back to where he came from. He shudders, not wanting to be alone.

"It'll come. It'll take time," Vedas says. "For now, you're still a man. It isn't, not even close." He clears a section of dirt with his feet. Crouching, he claws into the hard, soaked earth and levers up a metal ring in the ground. The panel opens with a loud creak. He gestures for Amur to look.

In the iron box are the knife and glove, separated by a partition.

Vedas settles into a flat-footed crouch over it. "You know now, what you're looking at—gods, or god-*makers*. The distinction is useless." He stares down at the artifacts like he hates them. Nonetheless, his hand trembles over the armor, and it's not fear making it shake. "We don't talk about it—didn't talk about it. It's irresponsible to keep them here. But in whose care could we entrust them? Could anyone resist as we have?"

Amur crouches next to Vedas. "You won't, though," he says, not even wondering at his certainty. The story is in the armor, and he'll know it, he's already starting to know it. "Not anymore. Not after today."

Vedas sighs. "Yes. Soon. Too soon, too *much*, knowing what I've done, haven't done. And of course, with her gone..." His hand hovers over the glove and for a moment Amur believes he'll take it. "My reign will be brief compared to Adrash's, but in the end I'll reach the same conclusion. I'll give up on men, on the elderim. I'll relinquish the armor of my own free will, hiding it from the world." He picks up the knife. The breath hisses between his clenched teeth. "I'll reach a compromise with this thing, burying the armor within it before giving my body to the sea. Don't ask me how it was done or why. I don't remember. Don't ask me how the elderim found it, or why it's taken the form it has now. Maybe the armor will tell you."

Amur has stopped listening.

...the form it has now.

He thinks of Sroma; he sees her running beside him, tongue hanging out the side of her mouth. His chest swells with joy, and he is filled with worry. All at once, he wants to be away, feet on the ground of the real world.

The armor expands, covering his chest and flowing onto his belly, cold and seductive. He gasps; in an instant it has assumed this territory. Fireworks erupt behind his eyes. A spell crackles down his forearm, gathers in his right hand, an unnamable, awful thing. He snaps his fingers, dissipating the spell with a thought. Like *that*.

The armor retreats to its place upon his chest, and he understands his power is diminished somewhat as a result. It is wondrous, this relic, and he wants more of it.

Vedas watches him. He shakes his head. "All that time—

imagine if your prince knew what treasures he possessed, if any of them knew. Arrogance, or lack of imagination." He looks at the house. His wife and son's house. He bows his head. "It's our own fault. We never really thought of them as people. We hurt them with our selfishness, our carelessness. And now look at the world."

He stands. "This Dorone, he's no different from any other. Just an *inheritor*. You needn't fear him." He looks down at Amur, eyes blanked to white and glowing softly. Sroma is a fierce shadow in his hand. "*This*, however."

Amur flexes his tingling fingers and rises. The world possesses a clarity now, one that he knows won't fade unless he allows it to fade, and it seems wild that he ever had trouble understanding it, any of this. It's not complicated. Take care of her. He will take care of her.

"I don't have the words," he says, "and I won't hurt her."

"Her." Vedas chuckles and gazes overhead.

The clouds have drifted clear of the sky above them. An odd constellation, straight as an arrow, spans a portion of open sky. Amur focuses on one of the stars until it resolves into a spinning cage, a man-made thing as massive as a thousand mountains. He examines a few others. Each is an artificial construct, a bomb poised over the world. Adrash's doing.

"Allow me doubt about these *words*," Vedas says. "Words aren't what binds us to the armor. We are the will and Sroma is the companion, the tool. Are you its master?"

"Her," Amur says. He shakes his head. The question is preposterous.

Vedas sighs. "When you hold a knife, are you in control of it? You don't ask it to cut, do you?" He positions both hands underneath Sroma, cradling her pitchblack length. She quivers, collapsing into a ball. Vedas takes her in one hand and shapes with the other, pressing his fingers into her yielding blackness. Anyone can see he's no artist; his fingers are just finding a shape that already exists within her.

A black dog.

"Of course not," Vedas says. "And if it's your enemy's knife, you take it and it's yours."

Amur stares, compelled to reach for her but resisting. "No."

Vedas purses his lips. He furrows his brow. He looks like he can't believe Amur's stupidity.

"If it's not yours, it'll be his."

"She," Amur says. He laughs suddenly. He doesn't remember why he's laughing and there's a new thing in the air. Not a smell. An end. His fingers and toes tingle. The armor tells him they can go whenever he likes. It flows upon his body, enveloping him, and the feeling within it is *certainty*—the assurance of his own power, the inviolability of this second skin, its connection with everything around him. As if his body itself is an eye, an ear, a nose. A conduit.

For a moment, he stands radiant in the moonlight, an idol of white stone. The desert fills his body; he closes his radiant eyes, keeping it inside. His home. Vedas's home.

He stands in the yard of a man who died millennia ago—a man who lived this moment, who became a god, who knows loss better than anyone. He is filled with Vedas Tezul, with the man's remorse and compassion.

(Godkiller, they called him in the old-old days, when he had ascended into the sky, more brilliant than any star or planet. Generations raised their children under his constant light. A long time. Not so long.)

He's tempted to think about this more. But he'll know all the stories soon, without even pushing, everything Vedas knows, everything Adrash knows. There is so much time, the armor assures him.

One question.

:What do I do with them?:

Vedas looks into the mesquite tree. He looks into the clearing sky. "It will humble the elderim, simply having to share. Give them some problems to solve. They were good, too, once. We all were. The world was beautiful for a while, cousin, it really was. A short, short while. It might have been a lie. I might not have really *seen*, you know? But I remember it. It was a time when I gazed upon them and felt such pride, such joy. I gazed upon *all* of them."

Amur touches right index finger and thumb to temple.
:Be with you.:

Vedas squints quizzically, but after a moment his face relaxes. He breathes in deep. He breathes in the same monsoon air as Amur.

"With *you*, Ola."

Prota, Medile Sea
(Winter—47 years old—3 years old)

It is night. He sits cross legged on the beach. The armor rests upon his chest, pulsating with a soft white glow in time with his heartbeat. A halo of pink and blue stones circles above his head; he interrupts one stone's passage, making it wobble in flight. Curled up next to him, Sroma has one paw in his lap. He scratches her head softly. He runs his fingers through the scarlet fur on her shoulder—the relic she now wears, trophy of her kill. Another manifests as streaks of jade upon her right thigh. This fur is of a slicker, more supple texture, holding a splendorous metallic sheen.

He wonders what rank of elderim owned these relics, passed down through how many generations. He wonders in what style they wore their armor. He senses their Elder makers' signatures, cryptic and ancient beyond man's understanding. He thinks about how much she's taken from the elderim already, and smiles. He can read the signatures if he likes, but that will take time and he prefers to be here, with her. He thinks of Dansia, and hopes she is alive and well, that the elderim didn't do too much damage to the city. But Sroma knew where to go. He sees her running through the forest toward the city. He imagines her hunger, and smiles.

"Good girl," he says. He says it a few more times, drawing

the word out ridiculously. He focuses on her rather than what's coming.

She spreads out her full length, legs rigid and shaking, yawning hugely, steam rising from her mouth like smoke from a chimney. She makes a sound like *rrrraaooooww*. She presents her belly and he gives her a good rub. She pants like it's a summer day, and for a while he's reassured.

She yawns again. She gracelessly smacks her head down on the sand and huffs.

He smiles, warmed by the familiarity.

When the worry hits him again, he takes solace in the armor's composure. It speaks no words, imposes no sensations upon his mind or body, but he senses its workings as whispers not yet resolved into words, patterns he's yet to grasp. He doesn't have to pay attention to it, but when he does the armor's autonomic pedagogy reminds him of a good song, a challenging track you're only half familiar with—the way it is when it first gets stuck in your head. Pure promise.

Nonetheless. The worry hits him again, and he must fight it again because this is his life and his duty. He envisions her victory.

An hour passes. Two. Day approaches, starshot night fading to blue lucidity. The air is frozen still. The sun rises higher and higher into the clear sky, and still they wait.

The worry hits again. He envisions her victory. He closes his eyes and listens to the armor's song.

She lifts her head. The sky cracks. She jumps to her feet, bristling, nose in the air.

Amur stands and stretches, refusing to let his gaze travel skyward. He breathes deep into his belly, into his chest and limbs and head. He merely *begins* to think it and the armor moves upon him, forming a skin-tight helm that extends onto his neck, covering his back, buttocks, and thighs. It slips over his perineum, ticking, and cups his cock and balls in a cool, tight embrace. He shivers. Where it covers him, he knows near invincibility. His shoulders and arms are bare, as are his chest and belly.

Cocky little shit, the memory of someone tells him. He grins.

Sroma pulls her lips back from her teeth, her growl reverberating. Smoke puffs from her nostrils. On her shoulder the scarlet relic moves like a flame; on her thigh the jade relic moves in streaks, like arrows in slow-motion flight.

He looks up and acknowledges the imminent arrival of his enemy.

Dorone is falling from the sky, headfirst toward the sea. A tail of violet fire extends behind him, whipping from side to side, lashing the air. He is sealed completely in the scales of his armor, which flashes like a jewel fallen from the void. As he nears the unyielding surface of the sea, he levels out and speeds toward shore. Twin wakes of seawater rise, foaming and spraying, to either side of him.

In moments, he will be here.

Amur's irises fade and his eyes become pure golden white; they become radiant like the sun. His halo of stones spins into a blur. He stands ready. She paces back and forth behind him, her tail slapping into his legs.

Dorone comes to a stop above the beach, righting himself a stone's throw from them. His armored body, haloed by an aura of pale amethyst fire, is obscured through waves of heat. The sand beneath him ignites, fluorescing as it begins to liquify.

Amur notes that his enemy is quite impressive, and disregards it. He watches, mind blissfully clear. He doesn't summon a single memory of this elderim, nor does he recall anything of his own life. If he lived another life, it was elsewhere, as a different man. He can choose what to include, what to leave out, when he thinks of anything.

His body feels fear when he thinks of this capability. He notes it for later.

Sroma rounds in front of him. Her growl descends through registers, tugging at his gut, making his inner ears itch. The massive bunched muscles of her shoulders jump and Amur smiles. He remembers her, her whole life. He breathes in the smell of her, and it's awful, and it too makes him smile. He remembers the Hound, how beautiful She was.

Dorone drops to the ground, landing with a graceful bend of the knees. The aura of flame is instantly extinguished. The scales of his armor retreat from his face, but he remains otherwise protected. Amur stares for a time. It is the face he's imagined—that fabulous unfussable silver hair, those perfect elf ears and cat eyes, that body. It's not important that Amur has imagined Dorone so many times, or that the elderim prince is still so beautiful, his features so compelling, for so much time has passed and it's only a face, a body. A man, an elderim, must be so much more.

Dorone is indeed beautiful. But he is not ideal, not for anyone.

Amur concentrates on this idea. More realizations come to him, all in a row. He knows things he didn't know only a second ago. He's becoming used to the armor's voice, but its song is still unknowable. Regardless, it moves through him; it changes him. The fear returns, and he understands he must humble himself, and never stop, lest the song overtake him.

:Sroma: he says. *:Calm.:* She looks back at him, over her shoulder. She turns back to Dorone, bristling. Around her the world wavers; if he quickens his perceptions enough he can see her *phase* in and out of mortal existence—she stands here and elsewhere, drawing power from places Amur cannot yet access. The smell of death is in the air.

Dorone clears his throat. "It seems I underestimated Orrus. And *you*, I—"

Amur gestures, shutting the elderim out. Dorone keeps talking because he still thinks he's making sound. Elderim and their talking. Amur ignores him.

Dorone can still say the words. He will say them, and they will be said to Sroma alone. Amur cannot prevent it, for the words are beyond sound, meant only for her. Amur sees them in Dorone's mind; he knows who first spoke them to Sroma, binding her in the ancient of ancient days. He sees the Elder, tall and awful, bones stretched out, skin taut as a drumhead, leaning over her knife form.

Fourteen words. Gibberish to him, even to the armor.

"Sroma," he says. She peers over her shoulder at him. Beyond her, Dorone has stopped speaking. He stares at Amur, at Sroma. Something shifts in his eyes.

"He's yours," Amur says.

She throws her head back and howls. Flames erupt from within her, spearing the sky, rivaling the sun. Thick grey smoke rises from her shoulders and back, coiling, snakelike. Her body shifts through planes of power. A storm cloud blooms in the sky above her. Lightning spears the ground around them continuously; they stand in a temple supported by pillars of light.

The heat is incredible, but Amur feels none of it. He smiles as she again levels her gaze, her fire, upon the elderim, who has masked his face and is falling back, toward the sea, a huge diamond shield clutched in his hands, deflecting her flames. He could have spoken the words already, but he was too preoccupied with his speech.

("Arrogance, or lack of imagination," Vedas says. "This one you know, he's no different from any other. Just an inheritor.")

From deep within, Sroma summons elderfire, a stream of purple lava that splits as it stretches toward Dorone. The radiant lines of molten dust coil like mating snakes, converging again before bursting upon their target's defenses. Dorone shouts; his shield turns blacker and blacker under the onslaught. Now he's lost the opportunity to speak the words because he's too busy defending himself. Words of such power demand attention; he must consciously summon them.

Amur senses the holes in the elderim's fusion with his armor. After hundreds of years, the relic still resists him. Dorone is not its owner, not completely, and he doesn't even know it.

Sroma keeps up the barrage, forcing her enemy back, back into the waves. The sound that comes from inside her is awful, like flesh splitting and cracking in a blaze, like stones being chewed into gravel. The ground beneath Amur rumbles. The sky cracks and the sea comes in counter to the tide. The lightning cracks into the beach around them. The sand explodes into shards of glass. He listens and this is music, too.

Her jaws snap shut.

Dorone staggers, falls in the shallows. He rises, but he is harmed, wounded badly. He is undoubtedly frightened, for this is not how the world works.

He starts speaking the words. She bolts forward.

Amur doesn't try to stop Dorone from defending himself. He quickens his perceptions to watch her instead: the *race* she makes of everything: the way her feet tear deep gouges in the sand, throwing up clumps behind her. She whips her head up and down, pouring on more speed, and she's moving so fast she outpaces her own flames; the twin trails of her arcane lava twist and sway to either side of her, still reaching for their target as they thin, dissipating into the air. She runs through a tunnel of light, through arcana of her own design.

His heart beats purely at the sight, and he needn't have worried:

The words mean nothing to her.

•

When she's done there's nothing left of Dorone, like he never was.

Most of the day is still ahead of them. He grins at her as she trots up, covered in Dorone's blood, panting, tongue hanging out the side of her mouth.

"Hey, girl, hey."

She drops it at his feet. A blue amulet.

"No, you take it," he says.

She swallows it. He laughs, and the relic appears upon her chest, a diamond of deep, nearly luminescent blue fur.

"Pretty fucking fierce," he tells her. He's decided not to add more relics to his own—to the armor, to himself. He's decided that Sroma shall have them as long as she wants them. She will eclipse him in every way. More elderim will die by their hands and claws and teeth, sometimes many at once. She must be strong. Perhaps they won't have to kill too many. Surely the elderim can reason it out, once they've seen. Men will be free. The elderim will be free. Equally.

"All that planning," he tells her. "For nothing. You did it all." He laughs and scratches her forehead, aware of his own regret. For a moment, he's angry at her for doing it, for taking the glory; but it's only a moment.

He stands. She follows him into the shallows.

The armor flows like oil, retreating to his chest. He pisses, long and satisfyingly, into the sea. The light of his eyes fades to a dim glow. The armor, an egg shape stamped on his chest, pulses like a second heartbeat, no longer keeping time with his body but something vaster.

He kneels. The water comes up to his belly.

"Sit, girl," he says. "No. *Sit.*"

She complies. She doesn't have to.

Slowly, murmuring soft words—"*good girl. who's a good girl?*"—he slips his fingertips into the bloody fur of her neck, her shoulders. He massages, loosening the clotted blood. She closes her eyes and her tongue drops over the side of her mouth again. He moves methodically, cooing to her.

"I try to leave, I try to leave, I try to leave," he sings. A face appears in his mind, a freckled boy. He knows where to find it, a music journal dated '201-02. Amid the reviews and doodles are other portraits, drawings of places, pages-long labyrinths of maddeningly complex weed visions.

"Agra," he says, and smiles. "Chora. Orrus."

His breath stops as he reaches under her chest and belly. She growls when his fingers rove over a newly closed wound. Otherwise, she remains still.

"Your face, now," he says, holding his hand before her nose.

She dips her head, allowing him to scoop water over it. He rubs her clean but avoids her left ear, a quarter of which is now gone, cut as though with a straight edge. Near the end, Dorone formed a blade of light to defend himself. (Was he tempted then? Did he cover himself in the armor and step toward her? He did. She didn't need him.)

"No matter," he says. "Scars are *so* cool." He lowers his hands and stares at her, into her eyes. She extends her neck, licks his face until she's satisfied.

"Good girl," he tells her. "*Best* girl. All done."

She stands, water sluicing from her sides, steam rising from her back. She shakes it off in a crystalline spray. He laughs, gets to his feet, and stretches, limbs shaking with joy. He looks down at her; she looks up at him, tongue hanging over the side of her jaws.

He clears his throat. "Do you want to go for a r—"

She barrels into him, knocking him over.

Sputtering in mock outrage, he stands. "Go!" he shouts. "Get it out of you."

Sroma's off down the beach. The man follows.

ACKNOWLEDGEMENTS

Thanks to Dominic Papa, Brennan Jernigan, and Steve Berman. Thanks to Jim Grimsley, whose work I read while editing and from whom I took inspiration. Thanks to Britton Walker of the B Boys for permission to use his lyrics as an epigraph.

Thanks most of all to Vinnie.

ABOUT

Zachary (he/him) is a middle-aged aesthete who digs homoerotic science-fantasy, punk rock, and pretzels. He lives in Arizona, in the high desert, in a broad, beautiful valley with a river running through it. He's had OCD most of his life, and in retrospect would have it no other way. He's written two other books but doesn't recommend them.

Feel free to contact him at jerniganzachary@gmail.com.